# Otters' Moon

ALSO BY SUSANNA BAILEY

*Snow Foal*

# Praise for *Snow Foal*

'I absolutely love *Snow Foal* – it's so truthful, tender and touching. A book to read in a day and remember for a lifetime.' Dame Jacqueline Wilson, author of the Tracy Beaker books

'A beautiful book with a big heart.' Gill Lewis, author of *Sky Hawk*

'How much my daughter and I enjoyed *Snow Foal*! It's a gripping, sensitively written book.' Jenny McLachlan, author of *The Land of Roar*

'A mesmerising new voice about a girl that deserves to be heard.' Joanna Nadin

'One of my most highly-anticipated reads of the year.' Hana Tooke, author of *The Unadoptables*

'*Snow Foal* shines out with compassion and understanding for the children at its heart. Susanna's writing is delicate and beautifully understated.' Julia Green

'A tender, lyrical tale for a cold winter's night that will lift the spirits and warm the heart.' Steve Voake

# Otters' Moon

## SUSANNA BAILEY

### EGMONT

# EGMONT
*We bring stories to life*

First published in Great Britain in 2020 by Egmont Books

An imprint of HarperCollins*Publishers*
1 London Bridge Street
London SE1 9GF

ISBN 978 1 4052 9496 6

A CIP catalogue record for this title is available from the
British Library

www.egmontbooks.co.uk

70522/001

Printed and bound in Great Britain by CPI Group

Typeset by Avon DataSet Ltd, Arden Court, Alcester, Warwickshire

*For my own amazing 'islanders': my children,*
*Ali, Joe, Josh, Emma-Marie and Oli.*
*With an ocean of love.*

# ONE

When we came to the island it was summer, but summer stayed behind on the mainland.

There's a chill in the air here. The sort of chill that runs through you when something is about to happen. Something bad. We *have* had blue skies – the kind of blue skies a little kid would paint, only without the yellow sun in the corner. If we see the sun at all, it's pale and half-hearted. Like *it* doesn't want to be here either.

I was *kind* of looking forward to all the 'fresh air and outdoor stuff' Mum kept on about when she sold me this Scottish island holiday. When she said the house was a stone's throw from the beach. I saw rolling waves; warm, golden sand. Kids that would be made up to have a boy from London come and liven up their boring island life. Well, true, the house is near the beach. It's all by itself on the clifftop, overlooking the bay. But the sand here is malevolent, full of tiny sharp edges to cut your feet. And it's more grey than golden. The sea stings your eyes and it's too still. Like it's holding its breath. Waiting.

As for the local kids, they're not interested in making friends. They just nudge one another and look away when they see me coming. Or whisper behind their hands. Not the kind of whispering the girls back at school go in for – this is different. It's like they know something.

Something *I* need to know, too.

But yesterday I did meet a girl with something to say.

She's sitting on the patchy grass outside our fence, staring out to sea and flicking pebbles over the edge of the cliff.

I risk a 'hello.' She carries on throwing and staring. I stand there, scuffing at the grass with the toe of my trainer, wondering whether she heard me over the whine of the wind. Whether to try again.

Wondering why she's here and whether *she's* in need of company, too.

My throat feels dry. She's probably just another unsociable islander. I could look pretty stupid here. I pick up a white pebble, weigh it in my palm; decide to give her the benefit of the doubt: I've had enough of one-way conversations with seabirds.

I sit down next to her and join in. Must be ten minutes and twenty pebbles before she speaks.

'You're him, then? At Cliff House?' She screws up her eyes like there is bright sun only she can see.

I nod. Ten days on this island and I'm as tongue-tied as everyone else round here.

Another five pebbles worth of silence.

'I'm Meghan. Meg.' Her pale hair lifts in the breeze. She pulls a strand of it into her mouth, tilts her head to look at me from under her fringe; points to the left side of the beach below us. 'That's my house – down there.'

'Where?' I peer over her shoulder.

'The boathouse.'

'You live there? But it's all boarded up . . .'

She looks at me again, a pebble poised in her hand.

'Grandad said a boy was poking around yesterday.'

I think of the old man I saw down on the shore, bent and thin as driftwood; his hair bleached and dry like the grass among the dunes. I had noticed his eyes as I passed: still as the sea, and blue. Bright, vivid blue.

'I wasn't "poking around",' I say. 'I was *looking* around. Looking for something interesting to do. Not that I found anything.'

Meg stands up. 'I have to go,' she says. She brushes sand

3

and dead grass from her jeans. 'Don't come by our house again, OK?'

'What exactly is your problem? You and everyone else in this place. Against the local religion to be friendly, is it?'

'Just don't come by,' she says, and grabs my arm. 'I'll come for you, OK? I'll come for you.'

'What makes you think I want you to?' I mutter, as she walks away.

'You do!' she calls without looking back.

I flick my last pebble over the cliff and watch it fall.

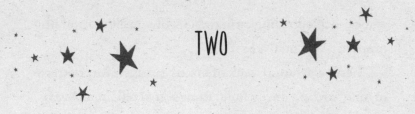

# TWO

Today, I am 'out of the house getting sea air in my lungs'. Apparently, this is just what I need. At nine in the morning. Apparently, it's not what Mum needs. She hasn't left the house in two weeks now, except to 'nip to the shop'. *The* shop. The only shop. But she doesn't even want to do that today. Still, at least that's an hour of my day sorted, getting eggs and beans. Another ten to go before it's dark enough to go to sleep. It gets dark early here. Even in summer.

The shop is some sort of converted chapel, with arched windows. One of them has a crack from top to bottom; its yellowing glass is criss-crossed with tape. The other is jammed full of stuff. What you might call a no-effort window display. Tins of fruit that look like they've been there since the war, a stack of 'Tom Piper' tinned steak (tinned *steak*?), bottles of cod liver oil. There's someone suspiciously like Captain Birdseye on the label – he has a pipe in his mouth, and he's puffing a massive cloud of smoke, while looking smug about the 'health-sustaining properties' of cod liver oil.

There's a pyramid stack of boxed 'Humane Mousetraps' in one corner. The whole thing's covered in cobwebs. Either there *are* no mice here, or the islanders don't go in for the 'humane' approach.

Inside the shop, ropes hang like coiled snakes from the walls and there are huge baskets of logs, buckets of coal, jet-black and glistening, sacks of green apples, and potatoes. (Most of them are green too.)

I find beans, a brand I recognise, thank God. I choose six speckled brown eggs from a blue bowl on the counter. A curled feather is stuck to one of them. I pull it off; blow it into the air; watch it drift from side to side, then disappear, lost among the apples. I wonder for the first time whether hens get upset when their eggs are taken away.

'You buying those things, young man?' A sharp voice from nowhere.

I almost drop the eggs, look round; see no one.

'Yes. Sorry. Just these, please.' I put my purchases on the counter, quickly followed by money.

The shopkeeper is younger than his voice, and, weirdly, dressed in a suit and tie. His hair is black, and too shiny, like it's painted on. He holds out what my mum would call artistic hands – long fingers, shiny nails.

'Thank you,' he says. He disappears under the counter, reappears with a battered tin box; produces my change. No till, then. My mum's brought me to some kind of Lost World.

'Don't suppose you know where I can get a decent phone signal?' I ask from the doorway.

The shopkeeper looks up, pen in hand, looks down; continues writing.

'That'll be a no, then,' I mutter.

Mum's up and dressed when I get back. Which is great. She eats breakfast with me. Which is even better. She 'hasn't been hungry' until dinner time since we arrived here. And even then, she pushes her food around her plate like it's something suspicious; slides most of it into the bin if she can.

'Leave the dishes for now,' she says, 'I'm going down to the beach. Thought I might try out my new camera. Come with me?'

'OK,' I say, wondering what *I'll* find to do down there. 'Great.'

The wind's dropped when we get to the beach.

That stillness again. Like walking on to a film set.

'Those old boats – see? Over there?' Mum points to the edge of the dunes. Close to Meg's boathouse. 'I noticed them when we got here. Covered in barnacles. Great colours. Think I'll start with those.'

I nod. Smile. 'Brilliant,' I say. 'Take as long as you like, Mum.'

Maybe she was right. Maybe this break will be good for her; help get over Dad. Help with whatever made her sad when he was still around. Maybe.

A seagull lifts from one of the upturned hulls, gives a loud squawk of protest at our intrusion. For a moment it looks like he's flying straight at us, but he swoops away, circles to the left and disappears.

I sit with Mum for a while, listen to the whir of her lenses, the click of the shutter: sounds I haven't heard for months. There's a leap of something light in my stomach.

I think of her bent over her laptop, engrossed in her images, hair glinting in the firelight, while Dad and I stick pieces of model aircraft to our fingers. Somehow, Dad always made the aircraft turn out OK. Even though there was always one piece missing. And he always got round Mum about the glue on the carpet. Always made her laugh.

That's another sound I haven't heard in a while.

We walk back to the cottage when we're hungry, have sandwiches and hot chocolate for lunch. Mum asks if I mind another trip to the beach when we're done, and I don't, even though it's boring down there. It's no more boring than everywhere else on this island. And when Mum gets up to clear the table, she moves just a bit more like herself. I'll take being bored, just to see that.

I help, put our leftovers in a bag for the birds. Not that I've seen any birds other than the seagulls, and I'm not sure about encouraging *them*.

On the walk back to the beach I ask when Dad's coming to see me. Mum doesn't know. He's busy, she tells me. But he'll come soon. He misses me.

'Right,' I say, wondering about the evidence for that. I push the wondering away. 'There's no phone signal on this stupid island,' I shout. 'Dad can't even ring me.' I kick at the rough grass under our feet. 'Is that why you brought me here, to get back at him?'

I didn't know I was going to say that.

'Luke, we talked about this . . .'

'*You* talked about it,' I say.

Mum stops; looks right at me. Her cheeks are pale again.

'Sorry,' I say. I look away.

'Me too,' Mum says. She shakes her head slowly, sighs. Like she's sorry about a whole lot of things.

It takes ages to get back to the boats. My feet keep sinking in the sand.

The seagull is there again, perched on one of the upturned hulls. It keeps its round black eyes on fixed on me; follows my every move.

Mum wanders up and down the sand for an hour, lifts and drops her camera. Gazes out to sea. She doesn't take any more pictures in the end. She blames the light. Not enough of it now. Too many shadows.

We go back to the cottage and this evening she's too tired to eat dinner.

When she goes to bed, I pick up her camera, look for the shots she took that morning. There's nothing. She's wiped them all.

My fault.

I punctured the day.

# THREE

Next morning, Mum's still in bed at eleven a.m. I take her tea, then coffee and toast, but she's not hungry.

Back to square one. Good job, Luke.

'Don't worry about me,' she says. 'Go off and enjoy yourself.'

Tricky. On both counts.

'I'll give it a go,' I say. I offer her the best fake smile I can find; hope she'll notice it doesn't reach my eyes and ask me why.

She doesn't. She just smiles back, nods; shifts further down into her bed. I hover, wait for her to ask where I'm going, what time I'll be home; whether I've got water and sunscreen and snacks. She doesn't do that either.

'I'll see you later, then,' I say. My voice sounds weird, sort of hollow.

'Bye, love,' she mutters.

'Sure you don't want me to stay?'

No reply.

I close the door. My insides are hollow too.

I head for the beach. The boats Mum was so excited about yesterday are partially obliterated by a layer of sand, scattered with strips of ugly black seaweed. I think about all the bits of Mum that got buried when Dad left: the bright, funny, loving bits. The bits that made her Mum. The Mum that would have given me the third degree before letting me leave today. My stomach twists. Does she even care about me any more?

I hate her; hate Dad more.

I miss them both.

I kick a shower of sand into the air. Another. I blink away hot tears; turn away from the spoiled boats and run in the other direction, towards the dunes. I fling myself down at the foot of the first one, lie on my back and stare into the stupid pretend summer sky. Wide grey stretches of nothing; vague splashes of watery blue, two thin clouds. A sky that doesn't know how to feel either.

I sit up, search for something to distract me. A pink crab hurries past my foot, its silly sideways scuttle surprisingly speedy. A childhood memory surfaces. I reach out, scoop him up and go in search of more.

I'm at a key moment in a race to the sea – six rockpool crabs ready on the pebbled start line – when the girl, Meg, appears out of nowhere.

'You seen my grandad?'

Her voice takes me by surprise. I make a stupid little noise that I hope she doesn't hear.

'Nope. Just me, a few crabs and one ugly seagull. The fun just keeps on coming on this island.'

'I used to do that,' Meg says, nodding towards my line of crabs, 'when I was little.'

I get up. 'Nothing better to do,' I say. 'How do you stand it here? I don't get why anyone would want to live in this godforsaken dump.'

She looks hurt, just for a moment. I feel a flicker of guilt. I didn't mean to be rude. On the other hand, I didn't ask her to interrupt my game.

'How long are *you* staying, then?'

I shrug. 'School's back in six weeks, but who knows? No one tells *me* anything.'

I grab my sweatshirt, shake the sand out. A crab falls from it, lands upside down, tiny legs and pincers flailing.

Meg bends down, picks it up and puts it on the back of her hand. It freezes.

'Shore crab,' she says.

'No kidding.'

I'm not in the mood for nature lessons. I should be

slicing up the pitch in the park with Sam, Luca and the rest of the footie gang. Or huddled in my room, jamming guitar with Jez, not a whiff of nature or fresh air anywhere near us.

She flicks hair from her eyes. Today, they're green, not blue.

'These mottled ones are the most common. They're camouflaged, so they can hide from predators,' she says. Her tone makes it clear that I'm one of those. 'But one in twenty are bright green, and some of the really small ones are yellow.'

'Wikipedia is a wonderful thing,' I say.

That squint from under her fringe again.

'My parents were marine biologists,' she says. 'That's why they came to live in this "godforsaken dump".'

'Thought you lived with your grandad.'

'I do. My parents – they – aren't around any more.'

'So, what? They just went off and left you here?' I laugh and immediately regret it.

Meg doesn't seem to have heard. She lifts her hand level with her eyes, peers at the small crab, still curled there.

'These guys can shed their legs to escape an attacker,' she says, 'and still survive.' She lowers the crab gently on to the sand, where it begins digging and quickly disappears.

'Handy,' I say. I pull my sweatshirt over my head.

'The long-legged spider crabs,' she says, 'they're the ones you want to watch out for. When the tide's just out, there's loads of them. They look like twiggy bits of seaweed. That's how people miss them. Especially in the mist . . .'

'Spider crabs. Yeah, right. I'm terrified.'

'Google them, then. When you get home. A bit like a big black daddy-long-legs, they are. They bind themselves with seaweed, create a disguise. Sneaky little devils . . .'

'Thanks, David Attenborough.'

'Don't say I didn't warn you,' Meg says. She turns her head, as if something has startled her. Then she just runs off; disappears among the dunes.

'The name's Luke,' I say into the air – suddenly sorry to see her go. 'In case you're interested.'

A gust of wind whips away my words. I spit sand from my tongue, pick up a large pebble and throw it, hard, into the sea.

I walk back along the beach, fitting my feet into the footsteps I left on my way out. That weird stillness is back again. The air is wet against my skin. And when I start to climb the rough cliff-side stairway to our cottage, the stone steps are slimy; slippery. Treacherous.

I look towards the sea. It has disappeared, erased by

grey mist. But I can make out two figures on the sand below, one reed-thin: Meg and her grandfather. Meg is pulling at his arm. He shakes her off, stumbles a couple of steps towards the sea. She grabs him again; hugs him close.

The sound he makes silences the seagulls circling above.

Later, when I try to sleep, his piercing cry mixes with my dreams. I wake in a sweat; lie there till morning, listening to the moan of the wind around the cottage walls and wondering what made the old man feel so afraid.

# FOUR

I give up trying to sleep at six a.m., decide to try emailing Dad. There is actually a connection this time.

I type quickly, in case Mum comes in. Not likely, on the evidence of the last few days. But you never know.

Hi Dad,
How are things?
I wanted to ring you but no signal EVER on
this island. Mum says you know where we are
but how does she expect you to get in touch?
It's like the dark ages here.
Mum's not taking masses of photos like she
said she would. Most days, she isn't even
getting up. I don't see why we have to stay.
I know you're busy but can you come and get
us? Me? Maybe I could stay with you for a bit?
Or even Gran's would be better than this.
Honestly, I'm going stir-crazy, Dad. And

school starts soon, anyway.

Be seeing you.

Love,

Luke

PS: What's happening with Boro? Any new players?

I read it through, take out the bit about Mum not getting up again in case that makes him not want to come. I press send. Nothing happens.

Typical.

I kick my shoes across the floor. They clatter against the bedroom door.

Brilliant.

I sigh. Thump the send button. This time, it works. Miracle.

Mum appears a minute later, squinting like she's emerged from hibernation.

'It's ten past six, Luke. You OK?'

'Perfect,' I say. 'Never better.'

She sits down on my bed. There are pink pillow-marks across her cheek. Her dressing gown is on inside out. I want to be angry with her; about Dad, about this island, about everything. But she looks like a little girl woken from a nightmare, her eyes all round and worried.

'I was just going for a wee,' I say. 'I tripped over my shoes. Sorry. Go back to bed, Mum.'

'Luke,' she says. 'Sweetheart.' She brushes my hair from my forehead like she used to when I was little. This time, I don't move away. 'I know it's not great for you here, not where you want to be. But I think it will help me. I really do. And when we go back . . .'

'When?' I say. 'When's that?'

'Well, you're back in school the second week in September, so . . .'

'We're not staying until then! No way. Mum, this place is doing my head in. I can stay with Dad. I messaged him.'

'You've heard from him?'

'No, but it'll be OK.'

Mum pulls at a thread on her dressing gown, twists it around her fingers; lets it unravel again. Her fingernails look like mine now. pale and bitten, ragged at the edges. Back home, her nails were always long, and painted an embarrassing bright red.

I wish she'd paint them again.

'Luke, sweetheart, everything's a bit – up in the air just now, you know. We're still not sure what's best . . .'

'Best for who?' I shout, standing now. 'Is anyone

actually going to ask *me* about any of this? I'm not some stupid little kid you can just cart around wherever you want.'

Mum is standing now too. I see that I'm as tall as she is. When did that happen? My fists are clenched tight. I sit down again.

'Jenny's baby,' Mum says, her voice quiet now. 'It's due next week. It won't be a good time at your dad's. I'm sorry, love.'

That's when I get it, this island thing. Mum's put an entire sea between her and Dad and Jenny's cosy new family event.

Suddenly, Dad's is the last face I want to see any time soon.

'Jenny's cooking sucks, anyway,' I say. 'I pity that kid of hers.'

Mum makes us an early breakfast. Pancakes and maple syrup. My favourite. I eat four to please her, even though I'm not hungry.

While I eat, the light changes. Grey shadows slide across the kitchen, suck out its colours. Rain scatters at the windows. Warning shots of worse to come, I know.

I go up to my room to get my warm sweatshirt; try to work out what on earth I'm going to do in this weather. I open up my laptop, check for a reply from Dad. Nothing.

Then I see him. Meg's grandad. Out on the cliff, way too near the edge. Hard to be sure, but from my window it looks like he's wearing pyjamas.

As I watch, there's a deafening crack of thunder. A flash of white light. It's the most exciting thing that's happened since I arrived on the island. The old guy just stands there. He's going to get struck by lightning. Or fall to his death.

I grab the waterproofs I swore I would never wear, run downstairs; pull on my boots at the door. As I rush down the path towards the old man, laces flapping, the light comes again. Disappears. Comes again.

Not lightning, then.

The old man is signalling. A huge lamp swings from one of his skinny arms. I call out, and he turns, his face skeletal in the lamplight. He stares at me for a moment, drops the lamp, staggers towards me, arms outstretched. His fingers claw at the air, reaching for me. They are gnarled and as stiff as twigs.

I freeze, not sure what to do.

'Stay still.'

Meg again. This time, I'm pleased to see her.

'Come on, Grandad,' she says. 'We can go home now.'

The old man smiles at her. Creases and crevices open up across his face.

Meg puts her arm round his shoulders; tries to lead him forward. He grabs my arm. His hand is mottled; dry. Like discarded snakeskin.

'David,' he says. 'David.'

'David's coming, Grandad,' Meg says, guiding him away.

'Who's David?' I say.

Meg looks back at me over her shoulder.

'You are,' she says. Her eyes burn blue.

# FIVE

I get to the boathouse before Meg and her grandfather. She must have taken him the long way round, avoiding the steep cliff path I took. Once I'd decided I was going to come. Anything's better than sitting in our grey cottage waiting for an email that will probably never arrive. And I'm kind of intrigued by this 'David' thing: who he is, why the old guy got so worked up about him.

I'm not sure I want to go into the house, though. Judging by the outside, it's going to be pretty rank.

I walk right round the building. The walls are made of strips of wood. Grubby white paint is peeling from them. The whole place looks like it's wrapped in dirty old bandages. Creeping plants hang in shrivelled strands from the roof. When I reach for one, it crumbles to dust in my hand.

There are boards nailed over every single window.

It's a house with no eyes.

I look back across the beach. No sign of Meg and her

grandfather, so I wander towards the dunes behind, hoping for a sheltered place to wait. Or maybe somewhere I can be out of sight while I rethink this whole idea.

Then there's this flapping sound.

Half expecting some mythical sea creature to rise up and snatch my head from my shoulders, I follow the noise, which is growing louder and more frantic by the second.

Brave of me, or a symptom of boredom, I guess. Probably the latter.

There are a couple of white twisted trees in my path, their branches locked together like the bones of battling dinosaurs. As I squeeze between them, the wind gets colder, lifts the hairs on my arms, bites at my ears.

There *is* no monster in the dunes.

I knew that.

But there *is* something.

A great bulk, covered in tarpaulin, nestles in the dip between two sandbanks. It's criss-crossed with thick ropes, pinned down like Gulliver. A corner of the tarpaulin has come free and is lifting and falling in the wind.

I make my way down there, sliding in the dry sand, and peer in through the flap. A putrid stench of fish and mould hits me.

I can't see too well at first; have to tug more of the

covering free, let in more light. There's a faint scuttling sound as I do. A crab drops from somewhere above my head, makes me jump.

It's a sailing boat. It *was* a sailing boat.

The old hull is slung with spiders' webs, thick and greying like layers of old rag. Barnacles cover the edges and sides of the boat as far as I can see. They're cold and sharp under my hand. I think suddenly of a shell-covered box my nan had on her dressing table.

She found me playing with it once, and that's the only time she ever shouted at me. After she died, when we were sorting all her stuff, I looked inside. There was a ring, and a scrap of hair, which Mum said had belonged to Nan's father. It grossed me out. But Dad got all sentimental, going on about how you don't really lose someone when they die because you always have your memories.

Ironic, really. *He*'s managed to get lost pretty effectively and he's still alive.

I pick up a twig from the sand, jab it among the cobwebs; tear at them, as far as I can reach. They're disgustingly tough. I clear enough to make out mast and rigging, folded down the length of the boat like the wings of a great bird that lay down here to die.

'Hey! Leave that.'

Meg is shouting, screaming, really, from above. I jump, drop the tarpaulin.

What the hell's the matter with her? I've had it with her making me feel like I'm in the wrong.

'Don't worry, I'm off,' I call up to her. I wipe my hands on my jacket. 'And I *won't* be back.'

The old man's face appears beside Meg's. He beckons to me and says something I can't hear.

'No, look, sorry – just come up, OK? Please. Sorry,' Meg says. 'I'll explain . . .'

It looks like she is reassuring her grandad, trying to stop him coming down to join me.

'Don't even know why I'm here in the first place,' I shout. But I scramble up the slope to join them, anyway.

'OK, OK, just, just come in, all right? It's too cold for Grandad out here and I'll never get him inside unless you come too. Not when he's like this.' Meg fiddles with the lock on their faded front door.

I'm not sure again and look at my watch. 'Actually, I *should* get back. My mum, she's – I said I'd do lunch.'

Meg ignores me. The door is open now, and she's reaching inside. Yellow light pours out. There's a warm smell, like someone's been baking.

I go in. I don't mean to, but I do. Curiosity wins, I guess.

The old man relaxes once we're all indoors. Meg helps him out of his jacket and boots, settles him in an armchair; fills a kettle. I stand there, staring around me.

The boathouse is bigger than I expected; brighter. There's a wood-burning stove like the one Mum wants, and a kind of kitchen along one wall. Pots and pans are crammed on to shelves and hang from hooks around a miniscule cooker. There's a cracked white sink. Dad has one like it in his new garden, with orange flowers growing inside. For salads, he says.

He never even cut the grass at our place.

The rest of the room is a cross between a small museum and a carpenter's workshop. One where there's been a small explosion. Wood carvings: intricate boats, tiny birds, a plane, various half-finished creatures and chunks of wood litter every surface. The dining table is covered in dusty newspaper. Curled wood shavings are scattered across it. More drift around the floor. A glass case above the hearth holds some sort of eel, frozen in mid-swim among stones and seagrass. On the window seat there's something horribly like a stuffed baby seal.

There are jars containing mysterious shapes suspended in cloudy liquid. The labels are old, unreadable. I'm glad. Really, I don't want to know.

You can't see the walls for photographs. Faded black-and-white shots, mainly: young soldiers; smiling girls with coiled hair; ships with guns; a toothless guy holding a massive fish over his head, a stiffly posed wedding photo. The bride has a horseshoe for luck. I bet she needed it.

The few colour prints are of schoolkids with gappy smiles and lopsided ties. One of them might be Meg.

'We've only got tea.' She's beside me, holding out a mug and trying to make room for a plate of biscuits on a small shelf, next to the skeleton of a lizard. 'Home-made,' she says. 'The biscuits, not the lizard.'

'Thanks,' I say, wondering if they're edible. I take one anyway, because I'm starving, and dip it in my drink. A chunk falls off and sinks to the bottom. I pretend not to notice, eat the rest in one bite. It's good. I scan the whole room again, still unsure about entering this weird world. But at least it's interesting. Being here beats hanging about with crabs. Or worrying about absent parents.

'This place is crazy!' I say, swallowing quickly. 'All this stuff . . . is it *his*?' I nod at the old man, asleep now, in his chair.

Meg holds her finger to her lips. She picks up the plate of biscuits, balances her mug of tea on it.

'Hang on a minute.' She opens a door at the end of the

room, flicks a switch, bathing the walls in a wavering blue light that makes them look like they're underwater.

It's her bedroom.

She beckons me over, flops into a chair by the bed; smiles at me. It's the first time I've seen her smile. She looks different. Which makes me more uncomfortable than I already am about being in the doorway of her bedroom.

I'm not exactly an expert on girls' rooms, but Meg's has to be unusual. It's full of books, neatly stacked. The walls are bare except for a bunch of childish sketches: stick people with huge faces and big smiles; animals with lots of legs; some careful pencil sketches of round-eyed, whiskered animals leaping and diving on roughly torn paper. There's a desk with an ancient PC, and, by the bed, a battered suitcase with a framed photo on top. That's it. No clothes lying round, no boy band posters. No nail polish stains on the carpet like my mate Jez's sister gets grounded for pretty much every week. No carpet.

'Have the chair,' Meg says, getting up, 'if that makes you feel better.'

'I'm all right,' I say. I perch on the edge of the bed and work on looking cool. 'So what is he, then, your grandad, some kind of collector?'

Meg flops back into her seat. 'He's lots of things.

He'll tell you when he wakes up.'

'I don't have much time.' I glance at the old man. If he's anything like my own grandad was, he'll sleep the rest of the day. I'm not staying in weird-world *that* long. 'Like I said, I've got to be back for lunch,' I say. Which is true. 'And I have to go to the shop first.' Not true at all.

'Next time you come, then. But the wooden things, Grandad makes those. The rest – the specimens and things, they're mine.'

She actually looks proud.

'That mangy seal is yours?' I say, irritated at the way she assumes I'll be back. Wondering whether I want to know this annoying girl at all. Even if she *is* the only one on the island who's shown any interest in me. 'And the Frankenstein's lab stuff – those disgusting jars and dry bones?'

'My parents' work, mostly,' she says. She sticks out her chin. 'I told you, if you were even listening, they were marine biologists.'

Her parents. Both gone. She told me that too. She didn't tell me why. Or where they are now.

I reach for another biscuit and bite into it, unsure whether to ask about them. The crunch is ridiculously loud, so I put the rest on my knee.

'It's the bonemeal that gives them their crunch,' Meg says. 'An old local recipe: puffin bones.'

I stare at her; feel as if I might throw up.

She laughs, forgetting to be quiet. The sound bounces round the room like a bubble.

I laugh too. First time in a while.

'Hilarious,' I say. I pick up a thick book from the pile nearest to me and flick it open. It's full of shots of what look like shells, or stones with slimy underbellies. There are excited blocks of pink and yellow highlighter all over the text.

'Offshore crustaceans,' Meg says. 'Fascinating.'

Not the word I would have used.

'You're seriously into this stuff, then?'

She nods. 'It's in my genes, Grandad says. My first word was "crab", apparently.' She leans back in her chair and crosses her legs. One foot taps in the air. 'What's *your* thing, then? We know it's not wildlife or the great outdoors.'

I shrug. 'Football and music. Mainly music. Guitar.'

'You any good? D'you have lessons?'

'My dad plays,' I say. I clear my throat. 'He teaches – taught – me.' I look away, in case the twist of loss in my stomach shows in my face.

Meg's foot is still. The air is still. I shift in my seat,

just to make something move.

'What kind of stuff do you play?' Meg leans forward, chin in hands.

'This and that. I was starting up a band back home. With my mates . . .'

'And?'

'Now I'm not.'

'Why?'

'Things got complicated.'

'What kind of complicated?'

'Just complicated.'

She looks me straight in the eye. I lean round and pick up the framed photo – there's a woman with hair like Meg's wearing a long flowery dress, a man with a tiny girl on his shoulders. They look happy.

'My birthday,' Meg says. 'I was three. We had a picnic on the beach: pink cake and everything. This massive seagull stole some out of my hand. Dad chased it for miles just to make me laugh, Grandad says.' She nods at the photo in my hand. 'I can just see my dad, hobbling back up the beach with his flip-flops in his hand and a silly grin on his face.' She looks away, stares for a moment at the boarded window opposite.

I gulp at my tea, my last birthday suddenly in my head.

I'd told Dad I didn't want him there. Him, or his guilty wad of cash.

When *I* was three, Dad took me to Disneyworld. Just him and me because Mum had to rest. We ate ice-cream sundaes for breakfast and I was sick twice on the teacup ride. Dad bought me a Mickey Mouse that was bigger than I was. He keeps a snap of me with Mickey in his wallet.

Well, he did. He's probably stuffed it in a drawer now, made space for a new memory. A new child.

'I can't really remember anything from when I was little,' I say. I put Meg's photograph back in its place.

Meg gets up, leans round me and pushes the photograph further back, turns it so that it faces into the room.

'You *could* remember,' she says, 'if you wanted to.'

I flip through the crustacean book again and pretend to drink more tea, even though I've drained the mug. My head feels kind of hollow.

'Where is your dad, then?' Meg says. 'Is he coming out to the island too?

'Look, I didn't come to – just tell me what you were on about with this "David" thing. I've got to go in a minute.' My voice sounds weird. I cough and clear my throat, pretend the tea went down the wrong way.

'We're just having a conversation,' Meg says. 'You

must've had one before. I talk, you talk. We get to know one another. Remember?'

She gets up and peers round the door at her grandad, sits down again.

'Come *on*,' I say. 'Spill.'

She folds her arms and sits up tall in her seat, just as the blue light above her head fades, flickers and dies. For a second or two we're in total darkness. Then the sea light recovers and washes over Meg's face, like a wave.

'Wind in the power lines,' she says. 'Grandad knew there was worse weather on the way. He's always right.'

'*David*,' I say. This time I'm the one not looking away. Even if the elements are in on Meg's avoidance tactics. Maybe there *is* something interesting here . . .

'Look, it's no big deal,' she says quickly. *Too* quickly. 'Grandad just gets a bit muddled at times. When he's tired. He thought you were someone he knew. Old people do that all the time.' She looks up at the light, like she's hoping it might do something to get her off the hook.

It doesn't.

'Who?' I say, remembering the urgent bony grip on my arm, the burn of the old man's eyes back there on the clifftop. The seagull-silencing scream of the evening before. '*Who* did he mistake me for?'

Meg sighs. 'Sometimes it's just easier, you know, if I play along for a bit.' The light flickers again. 'Like today.'

'But *who's David*?'

Meg stands up. 'My father,' she says, her voice like a full stop.

She walks out of the room without looking back.

I follow her back to the living room. The old man is stirring, shifting a little in his chair.

'I still don't get it,' I say, more confused than ever.

'Grandad needs to eat.' Meg's reaching pans down from above her head, clattering them on to the stove. 'I need to light the fire; in case the power goes off. You should get going. The wind's getting serious now.'

She crosses to the door, opens it a little, and proves her point. Sand is lifting, spiralling into the air. There's a threatening howl from the sea.

'It'll be dark when the storm really kicks in,' she says. 'Storms steal the light out here. Even in the middle of the day. You won't be able to see a thing – best get going.'

She hands me my coat. I'm going to protest, get more answers, but she's looking past me. Like one of us has already left.

Cold air slaps my face, and suddenly I'm worrying about Mum and that lunch I promised to make.

'I'll be back. Tomorrow,' I say.

My words are barely out before the door closes and I'm alone, sand in my eyes and nose, wondering how on earth the old man mistook me for a guy three times my age.

And why there had been such desperation in his eyes.

Maybe it's the meanderings of a tired old mind, like Meg says.

Or maybe those watchful, whispering island kids have a point. Maybe there *is* something about this island I need to know.

# SIX

It takes ages to get back to the cottage. The wind does its best to push me back three steps for every two I manage to take.

Mum's in the kitchen, peeling potatoes over the sink.

I hop on one foot, struggling to prise off my right boot. '*I'm* doing lunch,' I say. 'Sit down, Mum, OK?' I blow on my fingers, try to get the circulation going.

Mum turns, puts down the peeler and reaches for a towel.

She's been crying. I should have stayed home.

She lifts a smile on to her face, bends down to help with my second boot. When she gets up again, the smile has gone. Like it was too heavy for her to hold.

I'm not hungry any more.

'We could just have beans on toast?' I say. 'And watch a film, maybe?'

'I went to the shop,' she says.

This is good. She hasn't left the house since that trip

to the beach. Hasn't done much of anything.

'They had a letter for us. For you.' Her gaze shifts to the table. An envelope is popped up against a jug of artificial flowers. 'From your dad.'

We both stare at the envelope, like at any minute it might spontaneously combust.

'Dad doesn't do letters.'

'Did he reply to your email, Luke?'

'Probably wouldn't know if he had, would I? Like I said, the internet's rubbish here.'

'There you are, then.' Mum picks up the envelope by one corner; holds it out to me. 'See what he's got to say.'

I take it, fold it in half. 'I'll read it later,' I say. I shove it into my back pocket. 'Beans OK, then?'

I can feel the letter all though dinner and a rerun of *Liar, Liar* – which I chose because it always makes Mum laugh. Tonight it doesn't. It's the letter. I know it is. Waiting in my pocket like a threat. Or a promise.

I'm scared of both.

When Mum decides to run a bath, I go to my room, get into bed and stick my headphones in my ears. Jimi Hendrix does his best to drown out the thrash of rain on the window, but he can't stop Dad's letter burning my brain from the pile of clothes on the floor.

I rip out the headphones; open it.

There's only one sheet of paper.

*One.*

I scan it quickly. I read it again in case I missed something. I didn't.

My blood thumps in my ears like Hendrix is still playing.

Dad's not coming.

He doesn't care.

I crumple the letter and lob it across the room. It bounces off the strings of my guitar. *Dad's* guitar. The red Stratocaster he loved but gave to me because he loved me more.

I told Mum not to bring it here.

I haven't touched it. It's just there, propped against the white wall like a scar.

I'm not sure why now, but I pick it up; run my hands over the dusty wood. The neck is thin, delicate. It would snap if I squeezed hard enough. I imagine the sharp, splintering satisfaction of that. I could do it right now if I wanted.

I run the back of one fingernail over the metal strings. They're badly out of tune, but I start strumming – hard –

faster and faster, loving the mess of ugly notes; not stopping when the upper 'G' snaps and waves in the air as I play. If you can call it playing. My fingers have softened up. I haven't played since Dad dropped the baby bombshell and blew a hole through my hopes of him ever coming home. It hurts now: steel on new skin. But I keep on strumming. On and on. Until a second string spikes up and dies.

I've got red grooves across my fingertips. A pink scratch on my wrist where the strings fought back. The pain feels pretty good. Stops me thinking. I lie back on the bed, still holding the guitar. I'm drowsy, like I just ran for miles.

Without wanting to I'm remembering. How it used to be: me and the guitar. Drifting, getting lost; saying things I didn't know I needed to say, with picks, flicks and chord combos.

Feeling things.

Feeling like me.

Dad knows about that. Dad's been there.

But he's taken it away from *me*.

I push the guitar off the bed and kick it, hard, across the floor. It skids against the wardrobe, gives two deep twangs: the last words of an argument. Then it's staring back at me.

Still. Splintered. Silent.

It's the saddest thing I've ever seen.

When Mum comes in to say goodnight, I pretend to be asleep, so she won't know I'm upset.

She knows.

Her hand's on mine. Dad's letter is a damp ball under her fingers.

'Luke? What does it say?'

I draw my knees up to my chest, wish I could disappear. Wish Mum would.

'Sweetheart?'

'It says Dad's a loser, OK? Nothing new there.'

I move my hand from hers, pull my pillow over my head. 'Go to bed, Mum,' I say, although I don't think she can hear me.

When I come up for air, the pillow is soaked, the room totally black. I can still smell Mum's shampoo, but she's not there any more.

# SEVEN

I give up on sleep at the first signs that night is over.

There's a watery light creeping through the curtains, and when I peer outside, the sun is hanging sort of pale and limp on the horizon. The sky looks washed out after last night's storm. I know how it feels.

It's still really cold, but I want to be out of the house before Mum gets up. I know I should stay – tell her I'm OK after last night. Make sure she's all right, too. Like I always do since Dad walked out on that job.

I don't.

I'm just like *him*.

I leave her a sandwich, and a note by the kettle saying not to worry; that I'll see her this afternoon. Before I leave, I go back and add, 'Love, Luke x' at the bottom of the message.

I've got no idea where I'm going.

I end up on the cliff overlooking Meg's place, even though I've no intention of calling by like I said I would.

There's no room in my head for her today. I don't think she wants me around, anyway. Not really.

I sit down on the dew-damp grass. I pick at the cereal bar I grabbed for breakfast. It tastes of nothing. A big black-and-white bird swoops in from nowhere, red feet skidding in loose shale as he lands a few feet away from me. He begins a slow sideways approach, his narrow eyes on me, like I've stolen something that's his. I throw him what's left of the cereal bar. He's welcome to it. I slide down the steep wet path to the beach.

When I get to the bottom I look up. The bird is balanced on the cliff edge, wings spread wide like a dark cape. It's a show of strength. A warning.

Someone else that doesn't want me around.

I walk away. Away from the bird and away from Meg's house, down to the shoreline.

The sea looks as tired as the sky. Weak waves wander over crushed shells, bits of bone and slimy green weed: the spoils of last night's battle. I stand there, try to think about nothing, let the water wind around my trainers. The blue trainers Dad bought me – the week before he left us. There's a split in the right one somewhere, because my sock is getting wet and cold. Cheap gift, obviously.

The thinking about nothing doesn't work.

All I can see in this empty space is Dad and his shiny new life. Dad with his shiny replacement wife. Dad with his shiny replacement child.

It'll be a boy. I know it will.

I scoop up a handful of the debris on the sand and hurl it back at the sea.

A whole year since Dad left: over a month since he's bothered to visit. And that was just a call-by. With my useless trainers. And another of his useless promises.

All agreed, he said. With work. With Jenny. A long weekend here on the island: the two of us, father and son. Like before, he said. And a chance for him to check on Mum.

Before the baby arrives.

How can he not be coming? He *promised*.

How can he leave *me* to look after Mum?

He's an idiot. Who needs him?

I dig with the toe of my trainer, watch as the sand slides back into the holes I've made. In seconds it's like they were never there at all.

I'm not sure how long it is before I turn back, but when I do, the door to Meg's house is open. Her grandad is sitting outside, bent over something in his lap. I walk slowly, hoping to get back to the cliff path without being seen.

He knows I'm there.

'Had breakfast, laddie?' he says without looking up. 'There's herrings.' His voice is different today, softer. There's a smile in it.

'It's OK,' I say, and keep walking. 'No, thanks.'

Meg's head appears round the boathouse door.

'He caught them in the bay,' she says, 'while you were still snoring. Come on, city boy, bet you never had freshly caught fish in your life.'

She disappears back inside, and the old man signals me over. He brushes wood shavings from the rusted bench he's sitting on, his eyes fixed on mine until I join him. Then he turns his attention to his work again, scraping with a tiny blade at what looks like the beginnings of a boat. His purple-brown hands are dusted white. I can see the small bones, like scaffolding under a sheet.

'Herring boat,' he says, holding up his work for me to see.

Meg brings a plate piled high with golden fried fish and buttered bread. She kneels in front of us, holds it out. 'Still the best fisherman ever on the island, aren't you, Grandad?' she says.

There can't be much competition, from what I've seen.

The fish smell good, but they're still whole, with those filmy white eyes that follow you around from the fish counter in Sainsbury's. The old man takes one, tips his head back, and eats it; reaches for another.

'Better get in there quick,' Meg says. She shoves the plate under my nose.

I pick up one small fish by the tail. It hangs there, shivering. I think of the silver sticklebacks Jez and I caught in other summers. How we threw them back because the water stank of old socks; argued all the way home about who caught the most, or the biggest.

I want to be there right now, pushing and shoving one another on the canal path; laughing about nothing. Being normal. Not stuck here with a bossy nature-mad girl and an old man who speaks in riddles.

I can't eat this fish.

I notice that Meg isn't touching the food. 'Aren't you having any?' I say.

'I'm vegetarian.'

'Course you are.' I shake my head, wonder if it's too late to say the same.

The black bird is back. Great timing. He's growing on me.

He dives low, flapping his wings; tries to separate us from the plate of herrings. This time, maybe we *have* got food that's rightfully his.

'He can have this one, anyway,' I say, and throw down my fish.

He darts in, spears it with his thin beak, lifts back into the air.

'Black guillemot,' Meg says. '*Cepphus grylle*, to give it its proper name. There're hundreds of them on the island. Over the far side – those cliffs edged in white? Kind of a bird city. And the white stuff, that's bird poo. Centuries of it.'

'Proper tourist attraction,' I mumble.

'The birds were here first,' Meg's grandad says.

'Beautiful, aren't they?' Meg looks at me for agreement.

I give a half-hearted smile.

'Feisty, though, especially in nesting season.'

'Aye, lass.' The old man nods his head. 'Feisty, right enough. Folk say those white cliffs ran red back in the day.'

'What? Why?' I say. My bad feeling about this bird is getting stronger by the minute. I hope it's not still hungry.

'First settlers plundered their nests and put the young 'uns in their cooking pots. Birds would'nae stand for it. Picked 'em off, one by one, till they learned better than to come back.'

'So the red . . .?' I say, keeping a close eye on the bird.

It looks like it might have some sort of inbuilt grudge going on.

'Blood, laddie.' The old man's eyes are on me. 'Birds won the day. New ones all born with those red feet.' He scans the sky for our intruder. 'So folk don't forget.'

I look at Meg, who only raises her eyebrows in reply.

'Do people go there now?' I say. 'To the bird city?'

'Not since the herring fleet went,' Meg says. 'It's just the birds and the occasional skinny seal over there now. Not much else.'

'So the guillemots got their way?' I say, thinking that the ones I've seen still don't look too pleased. Seriously, is there *anything* to like about this island?

'Not really.' Meg shakes her head. 'They struggled for years. Their main food supply was pretty decimated.'

'Which was?'

'Herrings.'

I glance at the now-cold fish platter.

'Takers. It's folk like that as started it all.' Meg's grandad leans towards me, whispering. 'That's why it comes, so they say.'

'What started?' I say. 'What comes?'

'The Otters' Moon,' he whispers, and squeezes his eyes shut. Like there's something he can't bear to see.

'What's he on about, Meg?'

She takes a piece of bread and butter and waves it dismissively in the air.

'This place is big on stories. Island folklore. It's what you get when you're surrounded by sea.' She pulls a faux-terrified grimace. 'Monsters from the deep, ghost ships, selkies. We've got legends coming out of our ears.'

Her grandad turns, his eyes open again – but faded; older. And worried. Definitely worried.

'Catherine,' he says, peering at Meg.

'Grandad, tell Luke about the selkies.' Meg leans over and pats his arm encouragingly.

Catherine? I look from Meg to her grandfather. Both of them ignore me. Here we go again.

The old man is scanning the bay, one hand shading his eyes. He's trembling. He turns to Meg. His mouth hangs open for a few seconds, like he's waiting for his next words to arrive. Or afraid to form them. 'David's no' taken the lassie out there today? No' out tae Puffin Bay?'

No smile in his voice now.

Meg shoots me a glance. She looks like she's struggling with what to say too. She gestures me out of the way, sits down next to her grandad; stills his hands between her own.

'It's OK, Grandad. We're having breakfast. Herrings,

49

remember? Telling Luke about the selkies?' She nods her head in my direction, but the old man is looking the other way. He points towards the dunes.

A silver gull sails over them and swings towards us, screeching, as if we're sitting on his personal landing strip.

This place breeds feathered psychopaths.

It lands a few feet away and drops what looks like a tiny chick under one foot. It squawks pointedly in our direction, then spears the lifeless chick with its long beak.

Seconds later, a puffin falls from the sky like a broken kite. It scuffles to its feet; freezes: a small statue on the sand, all funny face and bright party clothes.

A clown at a funeral.

The child snatcher doesn't even look up from his meal.

'Unusual birds, puffins,' Meg says. 'They pair up for life and share the rearing of their chicks till they're ready to fledge. But they only lay one egg each year.'

I'm about to tell her to shut up when I see that she is crying.

'She'll forget,' I say. 'By the morning she won't even remember she *had* a chick.'

Meg doesn't reply. She walks over and kneels beside the mother bird, who doesn't seem to notice that she is there.

The old man gets up and totters towards me.

'Remember, laddie,' he says, pointing a bony finger towards the sky. 'Remember the Otters' Moon.' He turns and stumbles back inside the house, his back more bent than ever. But I'm rooted to the spot, staring at the duo on the sand. They sit there, heads bowed, for what feels like hours. It's like they're locked together. In something that can't be disturbed.

My stomach starts to rumble. The hard bench I'm sitting on gets harder by the minute. I shift position slightly, and the puffin comes to life. She glances behind; looks up at Meg and heaves herself into the air with a bewilderment of wings and ruffled feathers.

Meg watches her go. After a minute or two, she leans forward, digs with her hands in the soft sand. She scoops up the remains of the chick and buries it. She reaches for some pebbles, presses them one by one around the edge of the small, sad mound she's made. Then she turns and walks away, down towards the sea.

I stretch out my stiff legs, and head slowly back to the cottage. As I walk, I decide that Meg is as seriously weird as her grandad. But then I remember about her parents. And I think how, when Dad left for good, Mum cried for my nan as well as for him, even though it was six years since she'd died.

Maybe that's the way it works when you lose people you love. Like when Mum sweeps the leaves off the lawn, and they just blow back in with every new cold wind.

My eyes sting. This time, neither the sand nor the salt air is to blame.

I'm at the cottage gate before I remember the old man's warnings.

Where, I wonder, is 'Puffin Bay'?

And what on earth is an 'Otters' Moon'?

Maybe they're just creations of a muddled mind. But, thinking back, I get the definite impression that Meg didn't want her grandad to talk about either of them.

# EIGHT

Mum's up in time for a late breakfast the next morning. She drinks tea with me at the kitchen table. She smiles and nods at me over the rim of her mug, but it's like she's seeing something else all together. Or nothing at all. She's already heading back to bed by the time I pull on my trainers and doesn't even ask where I'm going. She doesn't say anything about Dad's letter. Maybe she's wating for me to tell her in my own time. Or maybe she can't cope with another of his let-downs either. Either way, this time I'm grateful for her silence.

She does ask me to bring more milk on my way home. Which means *she's* going nowhere. Again.

I set off for Meg's house. It's not that I'm desperate for her company, but the more time I spend with Meg and her grandad, the more questions I have. Focusing on getting answers is better than thinking about Dad and his stupid letter. Or worrying about Mum.

Meg is in the doorway. Her back is turned, so at first she doesn't see me.

'I won't, Grandad,' she calls, 'I *never* go there, do I? I'll be back before you know it, OK?' She moves inside the house for a moment; re-emerges. Spots me.

'I'm busy,' she says pointedly. She zips up her jacket, pulls a faded blue scarf from the pocket; uses it to twist her hair up on top of her head. 'See you later.' She spins round and strides away.

I'm still standing with my mouth open, trying to come up with a biting response, when she stops and turns back towards me.

'Don't be following me, OK?' she shouts. 'Find your own entertainment for once.'

Pretty rich, considering how she butted into my 'holiday' here; how she reappears when it suits her without invitation, demanding that I enter her parallel universe. But she's already too far away for me to make the point. Instead, I follow her.

Of course I do. She told me not to. And I'm wondering why.

It's hard to keep up without giving myself away. I lose her a couple of times in the dunes; have to climb higher, then slide down again once I've spotted her blue scarf bobbing along below.

After a while, the landscape changes. Dunes – and the cover they offer – are replaced by rocky outcrops, most of them rough, with sharp edges to snag clothes. And skin. My hands burn from the effort of heaving myself up, across and over them. My feet twist and slip. An ooze of blood trickles down my ankle. Meg is like a mountain goat by comparison. But every now and again she stops, and bends down, no doubt in raptures about some riveting example of wildlife. If she didn't, she'd have shaken me off miles back.

Another half-hour in, I see smears of colour up ahead: pink, green; touches of blue. I might be hallucinating from exhaustion. This island doesn't *do* colour.

I rub my eyes. The colours are still there. But there's no way I can stop for a rest. If I lose Meg, I'm lost too. I'm not at all sure I could find my way back alone.

I keep going.

The rocky landscape smooths; becomes one huge flat-topped rock – an enormous tabletop. And there's grass. Actual grass. A bit spindly and wind-blown, but grass all the same. And the specks of blue are flowers. Hundreds of them. They peep out from clumps of seagrass, their heads waving in the slight breeze.

A slight breeze. That's new too. On the other side of the island, the wind has only two settings. It's either full-on freezing, with teeth, or in that eerie film-set pause mode.

It's harder to stay out of sight here. And surely Meg can hear my heavy breaths behind her now. I don't want to give myself away before I find out what she's up to.

So for some reason I bend low. Like that will help.

Luckily, she doesn't look back.

The rock table ends abruptly. Meg stands still for a moment, peers up into the sky. Birds circle above. Seagulls, guillemots – hopefully in a better mood than usual – and shorter, fatter birds. Loads of them.

Puffins. They're puffins.

Is this where she lives – yesterday's sad little mother? Is Meg here for *her*?

I look down again to see Meg disappearing bit by bit from the cliff edge. It's like she's descending a staircase.

She is.

Steps have been roughly hewn into the black rock. Small pink flowers decorate the edges, crawl over the sloping rock face. But the steps look usable.

Meg's at the bottom in no time.

I'm rooted to the spot.

Below me, white sand stretches around a curved bay.

Yellow-topped rocks surround small pools. From this distance it looks as if someone has smeared bright yellow paint across some of them, Tango-orange across others. I see a strip of quiet blue sea – *blue* sea – beyond them.

I've stumbled on another parallel universe. A breath of life after the monochrome monotony of our side of the island. I hurry down the steps, keen to see more.

But once I'm down on the sand, the game's up.

Meg's crouching by one of the rock pools, talking to some of her precious crabs, I guess. She reaches between two rocks, tugs at something. When she stands up, I see that it's a large bag of some sort.

*She* sees *me*. Stares.

Even from this distance I know she's not pleased.

I stuff my hands in my pocket, walk towards her. 'Hey,' I say.

'What are you doing?' Meg's eyes narrow. A strand of hair lifts from her scarf, glints golden-red in the sunlight; wavers like a flame on top of her head.

I shrug. 'Wondered where you were off to in such a hurry.'

'Well, now you know, so you can leave. I've got stuff to do.' Meg shakes out the bag and feels around inside. She brings out a pair of stiff-looking gloves, like the ones Mum

57

bought for doing the garden. Only Mum's are still in the cellophane wrapper.

'What stuff?' I say.

Meg doesn't reply. She kicks off her shoes, starts to roll up the legs of her dungarees.

I sit down on a rock and unfasten my trainers. The sand is soft, warm between my toes. 'This is the place, isn't it?' I say. 'The place you're not supposed to be?' I make a show of looking around me. 'Lurking sea monsters, are there?'

Meg's reply is obliterated by a sudden squawking chorus overhead. Probably just as well. She tucks the gloves under her arm and stomps off along the beach as if I'm not even there.

I wander along behind her, my feet sinking in the sand. I have to squint in the sunlight. I start to sweat under my arms. Two more firsts for this island.

We follow the curve of the bay, edge closer to the sea. The sand becomes firmer underfoot. It's strewn with tiny seed-pearl shells – pink, primrose yellow, pearly white – blue-grey pebbles and curls of dark green weed. The breeze smells fresh, salty. Up ahead, the rock face down which we descended bends round to the left, juts out on to the beach like the bow of a great ship. It shimmers; seems to tremble at the edges.

Closer still, and I see them. Puffins. A great shifting river of black-and-white bodies, bobbing heads and striped beaks. I stop, fascinated. Two more come in to land, their bright orange feet splayed out like spoilers as they glide closer, then hover, searching for a space on the crowded ledges. Others aren't too keen to make room for them and there's a raucous squabble.

'No room at the inn.' Meg is beside me. One hand shields her eyes from the glare of the sunlight.

'You what?' I say, wondering, again, how she does that silent-approach thing.

'Nesting season, if you must know,' she says. They come every year. Used to be loads more too.' She sighs. 'Not so many fish for them to catch these days, so . . .' She shakes her head, twists her mouth to one side. I wait for one of her lectures. It doesn't come. But I'm pretty sure the puffin diversion won't save me for long.

She nudges me, points. "There, look. See those darker, smaller birds? They're young ones: fledglings.'

I copy Meg, shielding my own eyes against the glare, and spot a cluster of fluffy, scruffy-looking versions of the adults. 'They nest there?' I ask. 'On those small ledges? Don't the babies fall off?'

Meg shakes her head. 'They nest in burrows,' she says.

'There are loads in the cliff face. Sometimes they squat in old rabbit burrows. Every spring they come here – late on – to mate and raise their young. They'll be gone before August's out.'

*Me too*, I think. Somehow.

Meg is looking at *me* now, with her grandad's piercing blue stare.

'You *shouldn't* have followed me,' she says.

'Who says I did?' I stare back. 'Anyway, I can go where I like.' I think of her words back at the boathouse. 'Unlike you,' I add.

Meg peers up and down the beach, as if she's scanning for something. Or someone. Her crumpled bag swings on her arm, lifts and swells, in the breeze.

I follow her gaze; take in the soft sweep of the bay, the gentle sky, the sparkle of the sea. This part of the island is beautiful. Really beautiful.

Why on earth would Meg have to keep away?

'I don't get it,' I say. 'This place. Why would you lie about coming here? What's the old man – your grandad – so fired up about?'

'I *told* you,' Meg says. 'He just gets muddled about stuff; about past and present; gets things in his head, goes off into a world of his own.' That searing blue stare again. 'You

don't *ever* tell him we were here. Not *ever*. Understand?'
She turns and sets off without waiting for my reply.
Apparently, her word is law.

'C'mon, Luke,' she yells. 'There's work to do. And you've
just volunteered to help.'

The bay turns sharply inwards as we walk on, becomes
tucked between the huge puffin rock on one side, and the
rise of a smaller grass-topped version on the other.

'Cool,' I say. 'It's, like, hidden away. A secret beach.'

Meg shoots me a sharp glance. 'Needs to stay that way
too,' she says.

I sigh. 'I'm not going spill to your grandad, OK? You
don't need to keep on.'

'I know you won't,' Meg says, as if she really does. 'It's
not that, anyway. Not *just* that. It's –' She hesitates, chews
the side of her lip.

'It's what?' I say.

Meg waves away my interruption with a flick of
her hand.

'Otters,' she says. 'There are otters here in Puffin Bay.'

'Otters? So?'

'So they don't much like us,' she says. 'People. They
don't take well to intruders in their home.'

'Same as everyone else round here, then,' I say.

*Same as me*, I think, an image of Jenny, Dad's replacement wife, suddenly in my head.

Meg's hands are on her hips now. 'This is important, Luke. Otters disappeared from the island for years.'

'Sorry,' I say, although I'm not sure what for.

'And now they're back,' she continues. 'I've seen them – I watch them: a mother and two pups. So you can't go bringing anyone down here, or go on about this side of the island. If people come barging around and spook them, there's no knowing what would happen.'

I barely suppress a laugh. 'What people?' I ask. 'There's hardly anyone *on* this island! You're the only person that speaks to me. Well, you and your grandad. Who would *I* bring otter-spotting?'

'Exactly.' Meg nods her head. 'People here keep themselves to themselves these days. That's why the otters are back.'

'Don't tell me,' I say, desperate to head off another boring wildlife lesson, 'these new island otters, *they* have have red feet too, I suppose?'

'Look, if you're going to be an idiot, you can clear off.' Meg dismisses me with a toss of her hair, sets off at a pace again across the sand. She really should chill out.

But I need to keep her on side; find out what she's up to here.

I catch hold of her arm. 'Bad joke. Sorry. I didn't think. I won't disrupt the otters, OK?'

Her cheeks are an angry red. She shrugs me off, searches my face.

'Otters are amazing: beautiful, clever creatures. I suppose you know they disappeared for years from pretty much everywhere in Britain, thanks to people who "didn't think"? Selfish people who poisoned the seas and rivers with their careless chemical waste? Greedy people who stole the otters' entire food supply for themselves. Despicable people who hunted them down with dogs for their fur coats or – just for fun?'

I didn't know. Why would I?

My turn to nod, with my best attempt at a concerned expression on my face.

I look around. 'Where are these otters, anyway?' I ask. 'And how come they haven't got scared off by *you* hanging around?'

Meg wipes her forehead with the back of her hand, slows down. 'Because I'm careful,' she says. 'And quiet. I keep my distance.'

'I can do that,' I say, keen to stick with her; find out

what she's really up to. There's got to be more to this forbidden bay than a few secret otters.

Meg shoots me a withering glance. 'We're not going anywhere near them now,' she says. 'Anyway, they're probably sleeping. They're river otters – Eurasians. They mainly come out at night. Evening, anyway.'

'Right,' I say, trying to remember what an otter – any otter – actually looks like. 'So what *are* we doing, then? Whatever it is, can we please stop for a second first? I need a drink.' I swing my rucksack off my shoulder, thump it down on the sand; pull out my water bottle. The water is warm, not particularly nice, but I'm ridiculously thirsty. I offer Meg a sip. 'Got my own,' she says. 'For later.' She checks her watch, shifts from one foot to the other.

'Right,' I say. I glance at the bag billowing in the breeze, clearly empty. I wonder whether she's got a bottled water stash behind a rock somewhere as well; wonder just how often she comes to Puffin Bay. I don't bother to ask.

## NINE

The tide is a fair way out. As we walk further down the beach, further round the steep curve of the bay, the sand becomes cooler, firmer beneath my feet. It's still peppered with tiny shells and stones, but there are clumps of slimy black weed, pieces of bone-white driftwood and feathers of various sizes. I spot an upturned crab, its fat pincers tight against its pale pink underbelly. I flip it over, using the bottom of my water bottle. Its velvet-brown shell is cracked across the middle. It doesn't move.

'Leave it,' Meg says. She stoops, collects something half buried in the sand to her left. A flattened Coke can, somehow completely out of place here.

'It's dead,' I say. 'The crab, I mean.'

'Still,' she says. 'Leave it be.' She slips the can into her bag. 'Your first clue,' she says, pulling hair from across her eyes.

'Crab, or Coke can?' I say.

'Both, probably.' She hands me one of her thick gloves,

points down towards the sea. 'You'll see for yourself in a minute.' She speeds off ahead again.

I follow, squinting at the lift and ripple of the waves on the shoreline. There's a staggered line where they pull back and forth on the sand. Small rocks, perhaps, or bigger clumps of weed carried in from the deep.

It's neither.

Among the creamy froth deposited by the sea is a collection of rubbish. It stretches as far as I can see with the bend of the bay. Close to where we stand, half a plastic bucket and the neck of a glass bottle jut out from a pile of thickly woven netting. All kinds of debris are caught up in the net itself: more of the black shiny weed, a fish head, what might be a sock; bands of something slimy and grey. Despite the freshness of the sea wind, there's a terrible stench around us now.

I look at Meg. 'Gross,' I say. 'How –'

Meg's not listening. She bends, starts pulling at the net with a gloved hand. 'Old fishing net,' she says. She tugs at one of the grey bands within it, her face crumpled with effort. Or disgust. Both, likely.

She pulls it free, holds it in the air, and shakes it. It's a carrier bag, part of a blue supermarket logo still visible on one side. It hangs like a dead thing, water dripping from its folds. 'Plastic bags,' she says. She shakes her head. 'Forty-three so far since July.'

She's looking at me. I'm supposed to say something. I don't.

'Washed in with the tide,' she goes on. She flings out her spare arm, gestures at the spread of debris. 'All this washed in with the tide. All the time.'

'It's a mess,' I say.

'It's more than a mess. It's lethal!' Meg stuffs the plastic carrier into her own canvas one. 'Lethal for the fish; for all the wildlife.' She glares at me. 'Even you must know that; must've heard about this. At school. On the TV.' Her voice gets louder. 'Well, guess what? It's real.' She glares at me as if I'm to blame for all of it. As well as the disappearing otters.

'This is the reason: why you come here – to clear rubbish?'

'Partly.' Meg stoops, hooks something indistinguishable around one finger and waves it in my direction. 'Don't just stand there. Get your glove on. Make yourself useful.'

I hesitate. This can't be it: the great mystery of Puffin Bay. I didn't come all this way for a refuse collection opportunity. I look back the way we've come. Should I try to find my way back, do some exploring of my own, or hang around; hope there's more to discover?

I do as I'm told. For now. I bend low, try to extricate the slimy remains of a shoe from inside the netting. The smell makes me gag. I hold my nose and collect some broken bits of plastic, a water bottle, a bundle of sodden cloth, and something now green and indistinguishable from the sand. I throw them one by one on to the dry sand behind me.

Meg is picking her way across the froth-strewn debris like one of those long-legged seabirds that search for insects on the water's edge. She's holding goodness knows what against her chest. 'Put stuff in the bag,' she yells, without looking back. 'Don't just chuck it around.'

I pull a face and salute her behind her back. How did I get myself into this?

Meg strides towards me and dumps her own collection on top of the bag alongside my own. It's crammed to the top now. Hopefully, she hasn't got any more tucked away, or we'll be here all day on litter duty. Not my idea of holiday fun.

'We'll come back tomorrow, with more bags,' she says. Like I've already agreed. 'Earlier in the day.' She puts her hands on her hips. 'But we need to drag that old fishing net well up the beach, so it doesn't wash out again when the tide comes in.'

It's heavy. By the time we've heaved it far enough to satisfy Meg, we've both got red ridges across our bare palms. We weigh it down as best we can with small stones, wash stinking green slime from our hands and feet in the nearest rock pool. Meg's T-shirt and jeans are filthy. She smells like three-day-old fish. I'm sure I do too.

'How you going to explain that to your grandad, then?' I say, nodding towards her shirt. 'And your bag of gunge?'

Meg shrugs. 'No need,' she says. 'He's used to me getting dirty. We'll dump the bag in the bins by the shop. Takes ages for those to fill up.' She shoves her feet back into her trainers.

I do the same, then take them off again and brush sand from between my toes.

'Come *on*,' Meg says. 'Something to show you – on our way back.'

'What?' I say. 'Otters?'

After two hours of slimy sea spoils, they'd definitely be a bit more interesting.

Meg stays silent, her brow creased as if she's concentrating on something. Or worrying. I'm not sure she even heard my question. We walk in the opposite direction from the route we took to get here, carrying the bulging bag between us.

Round the twist of the bay, I make out a flat wooden platform that stretches across the sand towards the sea. Further out, there is what looks like a lighthouse, or part of one, on a platform of rocks. It pushes into the sky like a striped exclamation mark. It looks odd. Part of the section where the light ought to be is missing. I stop, causing Meg to do the same.

'Isn't that still used, then?' I say.

Meg shakes her head. 'Only by me. Sometimes – I like it in there. But not as a lighthouse. It's not really needed. No one sails into this bay. Not now.'

'Why not?'

'There are other places to land on the island. Better places.' She stares off into the distance for a moment. 'Safer places.'

I look at the satin-blue water, the smooth line of gentle sky above it. 'Doesn't exactly look dangerous,' I say.

Megs turns to me. Her chin lifts. Her blue eyes are narrow: seabird eyes; suspicious, unsure.

'What?' I say.

Her chin lifts. She sighs. Like she's decided something. Something important.

'It's changeable here. The weather; the sea. Things. They catch people out.' She draws in a huge breath. 'Mum and

Dad,' she says, her voice smaller; tighter, 'we lost them here – off this bay –'

My turn to stare. 'What . . . You mean –'

Meg nods. She plonks herself down on the sand, draws her knees up under her chin.

'Mum, she needed some underwater samples; some study deadline she had. Dad didn't want her to dive. Not that day.' She bites her lip. 'She said she'd be quick. She'd be back well before sunset –'

I ease myself down beside her. Not too close.

'She wasn't.' Meg scoops sand and lets it trickle away through her fingers. 'Back.'

I wait.

'Dad took Grandad's boat out; went to find her. He didn't come back either.'

I see her, not yet four years old, staring out to sea; waiting at the water's edge. Waiting for the bob of a boat, the wave of a hand. Wondering why they didn't come.

'God, Meg,' I say. 'I'm sorry.' The words feel ridiculously small on my tongue. I can't find any that don't. Both her parents swallowed by the sea. Just like that.

She blinks, brushes at her cheek. 'Wind's getting up.' She turns away from me, watches gulls wheeling overhead. 'We should get back.' She kneels up, reaches for her bag. 'Grandad'll need his tea.'

'Wait,' I say, my own voice scratchy, like the sand has got in there. 'Why – what happened – to them, your parents? Do you know?'

Meg gets to her feet, looks straight at me. 'No one knows for sure,' she says. 'Not even Grandad. Whatever he says.'

Then she's off, scrambling back towards the cliff edge, and I'm trailing behind again, feeling like there are cold pebbles in my stomach, missing my dad and wondering exactly what the old man thinks he knows.

# TEN

We wind our way between grassy dunes; reach a stretch of pebbled sand shielded by a few large rocks. 'Crouch down low,' Meg whispers. 'We'll stop just there. Behind that upturned boat. See it?'

It protrudes from the sand, like the discarded home of a prehistoric sea turtle. The part of the hull still visible is bleached dirty white by sea and sun. A worn wooden post stands at one side of it. As we creep closer, I see frayed fragments of rope there, still attached to a rusted metal loop.

Meg cups a hand around my ear, speaks into it. 'Lie down on your stomach.'

I sigh – clearly too loudly, given Meg's expression; nod, and do as instructed.

I prop myself up on my elbows, peer over the backbone of the boat.

Up ahead, a broken wooden platform leads a short distance into the sea – which is deep turquoise in the evening light. Dark lacy islands of seaweed float there. Two tall stones stand in the water, throwing low shadows on the surface. Another pair lean together at the water's edge as if frozen. Waiting.

Meg and I wait too. Feels like hours.

Meg lies rock-still. I fidget, reach for tiny shells and pebbles while her gaze is elsewhere, make patterns with them in the damp sand. Cold seeps into my bones. The sea creeps closer. An early moon lifts melon-white on the horizon.

The otters clearly have other plans. Or they know we're here.

We're wasting our time.

I shuffle; rub my hands together for warmth. I worry about Mum.

Have I been gone too long?

'Better get going, hadn't we?' I whisper. I point at the moon. We've been out for hours.

There's a sharp elbow in my side.

Meg presses a finger to her lips, signals ahead with widened eyes.

A whiskered brown face peers out from between moss-covered rocks, large dark eyes catching the light.

'Otter pup,' Meg mouths, her face alight too.

I hold my breath, watch as a slim grey-brown body emerges, pauses; sniffs the air.

A second, smaller pup bursts through the gap and catapults towards the first. They roll and tumble, a tangle of too large clawed feet and long, lashing tails. They nip at each other, leap in the air, playing just like my mate Jez's terrier pups. They make weird *peeping* sounds.

One of them breaks free; disappears. I ease myself higher and watch as its playmate scurries towards the sea after him. Or her.

Meg tugs at my arm, points at a group of large rocks close to the water's edge.

'Better view from there now,' she says and crawls towards them.

I sigh. We've seen the otters now. They're cute, I admit. But the sea is creeping towards us; creeping inside my trainers, cold and uncomfortable. I don't fancy hanging around, becoming part of another island tragedy: *City Boy Falls Victim to Island Curse*.

Mum would never forgive herself. Never recover.

I crawl after Meg. 'I don't see any otters,' I say. 'Let's go.'

Meg doesn't reply, just nods towards the darkening water.

I follow her gaze.

A sleek head breaks the surface, followed by a second.

There's the hump of a back; the thrash of a tail tip. A second head. Another tail.

The tumbling begins again. The otters leap and dive at one another, even more agile in the sea than they were on land. They take turns to dip below the water every so often; to reappear a few feet away, chattering at the other. It's like they're playing hide-and-seek. It's like they're laughing.

I forget about my wet foot, the encroaching tide. These little guys are seriously cool. Mum would love them. It might cheer her up a bit to see them; spark her interest in getting out to explore the island a bit more. It's got to be worth a try.

I slide my bag from my shoulder, bring out my phone.

Meg's eyes burn into the side of my face.

'What are you doing?' she hisses.

'Taking a quick video,' I hiss back at her. 'No law against it.'

'You promised,' she says, the hiss moving up an octave or two. She tries to grab my phone.

'It's for my mum, OK?' I say, twisting out of her reach. 'Just her. It's important. She won't tell anyone about them. And I can do what I like, anyway.'

Meg's on her feet, keeping low as she heads back up the beach. Her silent feet leave perfect prints in the sand.

No time for filming, then.

Great. I grab my bag, stuff my phone in my pocket.

'Wait,' I call.

She's halfway up a steep dune before I catch up with her.

'Meg,' I say, trying to catch my breath. 'Meg, can you just . . . stop?'

She speeds up. Apparently sliding sand is no hindrance for her.

Not true for me.

I try to catch hold of her sleeve, end up doing a kind of stomach-sledge move in the other direction.

That gets her attention. A glance over her shoulder in the half-light, anyway. She doesn't stop. I might have several broken bones for all she knows.

I scrabble to my feet, spit sand from my tongue. 'Wait, Meg, OK?' I'm shouting now. 'Just listen a minute. For once.'

She spins round, hands on hips. 'Not interested,' she says. 'Should never have brought you here. Should've known.'

'What?' I say, level with her now.

Her cheeks are scarlet. 'I *told* you,' she hisses. 'You *can't* let on about the otters. Not to *anyone*.' She shakes her head. 'City people. You're all the same.' Something glints on her cheek. 'Stupid of me,' she says. 'Trusting you with something important. Something that actually *matters*.'

I pull a face that's probably lost on her in the dim light. She sets off again, like I'm not even there. Fury gives me a spurt of energy. I push in front of her.

'You don't know *anything* about me,' I say, right into her face. 'It's always about you. The things *you* care about. Things you worry about. Your precious wildlife. Your precious grandad. You act like you're the only one in the world who's got family worries. The only one who's lost someone –'

My voice cracks. I swallow. 'The only one who's sca—'

Meg's eyes hold my own. She opens her mouth to speak. Tears burn behind my eyes.

'Forget it,' I say, turning my back on her. 'Let's just get home.'

We walk in silence for a while, the bubble of otter excitement well and truly burst.

Meg doesn't forge ahead for once, keeps shooting glances at me. I gaze in the other direction, afraid of those beady bird eyes of hers. In the half-light trees bend towards the sea – now just a whisper in the distance.

'Your mum,' she says. 'What's she like?'

I focus on the feel on the ground beneath my feet; the roughness of sanded seagrass has given way to softer, lusher grass. It tickles my shins as I move.

'Only, you don't really mention her much.'

'She's a photographer,' I say.

'Yes, but what's she *like*? Do you guys get along? How come I don't see her out and about?'

I bend, snatch up a long blade of grass, chew on it. Its bitter, lemony taste stings my tongue, mingles with the words balled up in my throat. Words I can't speak out loud.

Suddenly I regret plaguing Meg with questions about her life; get why she's not keen on giving answers.

Words, they make things real.

I shrug. 'She's great,' I say. 'She's just, you know, my mum. No one hangs out with their mum.'

Meg falls silent again. I bite my lip; think how she'd give pretty much anything to hang out with *her* mum again. How I would too, if I still knew how to find her.

'Sorry,' I say.

I don't think she hears me.

After a while, the salt smell of the sea gives way to something more mulchy, earthy and damp. I hear the run of water over stones, gentle this time.

'River up ahead,' Meg says, like she's inside my head. 'Well, burn, to be exact.'

She lowers her voice. 'See those willows?' she asks. 'The otters rest there during the day sometimes. On that fallen trunk, see? It's partly eaten away in the middle but camouflaged with overhanging branches. An otter couch, it's called.'

I can't see much now, make a move to get closer for a better look.

'No,' Meg says. 'Stay back. If the mum picks up your fresh scent on the ground, she might abandon the couch. You could be a threat to her young. She might even abandon them. Like I said, otters are easily spooked.'

'Right,' I say. I step back. Maybe Meg's forgiven my otter transgression. I don't want to upset her all over again. Or worry her precious otters. 'It doesn't look all that safe here, anyway,' I say, peering past the three solitary cascading trees. 'Not for giving birth in.'

Meg shakes her head. 'Otter mums are cleverer than that. They don't nest near rivers – too many possible predators around. She brought the babies here once they outgrew the nest – the holt – they were born in, so she could start teaching them to swim and hunt for food. The holt's in the woods. It was hard to find. Otter mums are super-protective.' She tugs at my sleeve. 'C'mon,' she says.

'Where's the otter dad in all this?' I ask, as we set off again.

'Otter dads don't hang around.' Meg fishes in her

pocket, offers me a sweet wrapped in purple foil. 'They play no part in rearing their young,' she says, sucking noisily on what smells like a mint. 'The sire of the two we saw will have other litters dotted around the island. He'll be kingpin around here.'

'So he just clears off; leaves the mothers to it? They've got to look after the little ones, hunt for them, teach them – everything?'

'Yep.'

'Typical,' I say.

I shove Meg's sweet into my mouth, crack it in two and crush it to oblivion between my teeth.

# ELEVEN

Meg invites me to come in for for tea. I'm not sure why I accept. Partly because I'm still intrigued by her grandad's mysterious moon warnings and hoping he might say more. Partly because I'm avoiding another anxious mealtime with Mum.

Once I'm inside the boathouse, I wonder why I bothered. Other than fussing about whether her grandad is warm enough, Meg falls silent. The old man just squints at me, gives a brief nod, apparently oblivious to the stench of fish we've brought in with us.

Meg washes her hands in the kitchen sink, disappears into her room, presumably to change. I open a couple of doors, find a tiny bathroom. Well, more of a cupboard with a shower and toilet – both antiques, but clean. Gleaming. No sink. The shower makes an ear-piercing screech when I turn it on, spits hot water in frantic bursts. I manage to clean off my hands and arms, soak the front of my T-shirt in the process.

Meg's at the stove when I come out. She glances over her shoulder, raises an eyebrow at me. I perch on the window seat while she cooks, keeping my distance from the stuffed seal. I listen to the hiss of bacon in the pan, the muffled sigh of the sea, the sudden whip of wind around the boathouse. It's building quickly; pushing through the thin walls, lifting the hairs on my arms. The windowpanes rattle behind the rough boarding. The warmth of Puffin Bay seems a world away. This island really can't make its mind up what kind of place it's supposed to be.

Questions about the tragedy in Puffin Bay tumble round my head like wind-blown leaves. How could two people who knew the island, knew the seas here, get things so wrong out there? What's with the disused lighthouse – why does no one sail into that apparently peaceful bay any more? Surely there was a proper investigation?

Of course Meg doesn't want to talk about it. I shouldn't try to make her. I should leave it alone. But I'm starting to feel uneasy about this island. There's something in the air. Something in the old man's warnings –

Maybe I *could* ask about the boarded windows. I mean, who does that? Come to think of it, who decides to live in a flimsy boathouse on an island that stole half their family? Surely Meg and her grandad have a proper home somewhere. One less like a house of sticks.

I glance at Meg. She's slicing bread – hacking at it, actually. Now isn't the time to ask.

The old man's not interested in lunch. He nods his thanks at Meg but leaves his plate of thick sandwiches to go cold, works away at a new chunk of pale wood. Tiny shavings collect in his lap. His brow is creased with concentration. It looks like that's been carved too.

I watch him work as I wolf down salty bacon inside slices of thick fresh bread. I try to decide what he's making. A seal?

A large otter?

I wonder whether he knows I'm here. And if he does, who he thinks I am today.

When I get up and take my empty plate to the sink, he speaks.

'Want to have a go, laddie?' he says. 'C'mon, I'll show ye.' He brushes shavings from the chair beside him at the table. His eyes are on me: this time they're bright and clear. Full of light.

I feel Meg's eyes on me too. I glance at her; sit down next to her grandad. He blows dust from the carving he's been working on; puts it to one side. Close up I see that there's the beginnings of a face at one end. A human face.

Not a seal or an otter, then.

'What is it?' I say.

He laughs. A surprising rippling laugh. Water over pebbles.

He shakes his head. 'What do they teach bairns on the mainland these days?'

'Nothing interesting, that's for sure.' Meg drags the rocking chair over to the table; flops down in it. She's back.

Her grandad puts his crinkled hand on hers for a moment.

Meg looks at me. Sighs. 'Old fight,' she says. 'Don't go there.'

The old man holds out the unfinished carving. 'This here's a selkie,' he says.

I take it; run my fingers from the half-formed face, down a smooth rounded back along a sort of divided tail. I think again of the seals I've seen in Puffin Bay, heaving their bulky bodies over the rocks, their thick flippers, their rudder-like tails.

I'm none the wiser. I look up. Shrug.

'Cunning changeling creatures, that's what they are. Curse of the sea.' The old man holds out his hand for the half-finished model. 'You don't want tae meet one, laddie. Watch yoursel' off these shores.'

Meg's turn to laugh. 'Don't scare city boy, Grandad,' she says.

The old man doesn't reply. He points a bony finger in the direction of a pile of books in the corner. He looks at me, nods, stares today's bright blue stare. 'The big one. At the bottom. Fetch that one over here.'

It's a heavy book, the pages yellow-brown at the edges. The cover is faded, white with dust. I can make out a blustery seascape; some scratched gold lettering in the centre: *SPIRITS OF THE SEAS: LEGENDS OF THE SCOTTISH ISLES.*

I hold it out to the old man, but he waves it away.

'Tek it, laddie,' he says. 'Read and learn. Read and learn.' He winks at me; laughs his watery laugh; starts searching among small pieces of wood at the back of the table.

'Thank you,' I say. I clutch the book to my chest, inhale its musty scent and wonder whether that's my cue to leave. I glance at Meg for help. She doesn't offer any. Just picks up the plate of untouched sandwiches and walks away.

'I'll make you some more, Grandad,' she says. 'And this time, you've got to eat them.'

He smiles at Meg, nods. He picks up a pale chunk of sea-washed wood. 'Now then, laddie,' he says, 'want tae have a go?'

He hands me his short, fat knife. I turn it over in my palm, feel the warmth of the worn black handle, the cool slide of the silver blade.

The old man reaches out; folds his paper-dry fingers over mine. 'Like this,' he says. 'That's it. That's right.'

I reach for the new piece of wood, keen to feel the pull of sharp steel against it; to make a first cut.

'No,' the old man says, his hand hovering on mine again. 'Look at the wood; just look a while.'

I look. I have no idea what I'm looking *for*.

'Look and see, laddie,' he says. 'Look and see. Be patient, be still; see what's there, waiting to be found.' He looks right into my eyes. Right into the middle of me.

'Things a boy needs to learn, laddie. Things for life, no' just for wood.'

I put down the knife; turn the driftwood over in my hands; stare harder. I close my eyes – partly because I don't know what else to do or say. I wonder about the tree my chunk of wood came from; imagine it snatched away by a storm, tumbling with the waves, travelling with the tides; tossed on to the island, like the remains of a bony meal. I think of the old boat I saw, lying like a broken bird behind the house.

I look up at the old man. 'A boat,' I say. 'That fishing

boat outside, with masts and rigging and everything. Can I make that?'

He looks at the wood in my hand, looks at me. Looks past me, the colour bleached from his eyes.

I follow his gaze. There's nothing. Just a boarded-up window staring blankly back at us.

'The Otters' Moon,' he whispers. 'I *told* them.' He turns his empty eyes on me: 'It's coming back, laddie,' he says. His voice trembles. 'It's coming back for *you* . . .'

Meg hurries forward with a blanket. 'Grandad's tired,' she says. 'I knew I should've made him eat his lunch.' She tucks the blanket around his knees, pulls it up over his arms. 'There you go, Grandad. Have a bit of a nap.'

The old man fixes her with his hazy gaze; squints at her under a furrowed brow. Opens his mouth; says nothing. After a moment, he picks up his knife and the half-finished carving; makes long, smooth strokes down the length of its body.

I swear he's forgotten his warning. Forgotten I'm even there.

I glance at Meg. Her face is tight; closed.

I hesitate. But I have to ask.

I lower my voice to a whisper, choose my words carefully.

'What did he *mean*?' I say. 'You going to tell me?'

Meg shakes her head. 'He's tired. I said. You need to go now. I've got jobs to do.'

She scoops up the book of sea tales, shoves it into my arms. She opens a cupboard, takes out a scratched wooden broom; begins gently sweeping around the old man's feet. 'Come again tomorrow,' she says, her eyes on her grandad, whose head has dropped on to his chest now. 'For the shore clearance. I can show you some caves as well if you want.'

I think of the tiny girl waiting and wondering on the shoreline for parents that never came home. I can't press her for answers right now. But I need some soon. This is starting to feel personal.

'Caves?' I say. 'Really? What time?'

She shrugs. 'Depends,' she whispers. 'On the tide times. They're not always predictable this time of year. I'll call for you.' She turns her back, carries on sweeping.

I go, closing the door softly behind me.

The wind whisks tiny curls of wood from my sleeve. As I watch them spin away, I think about how the old man was with me one minute and gone the next. How in that moment when he didn't know his own granddaughter, his hands remembered how to shape life from a piece of long-dead wood.

And how the mention of that disused fishing boat triggered his fear; brought us back to the mysterious Otters' Moon.

Whatever that might be.

I wrap my arms around his book of island legends, keeping it tightly closed against the tug of the wind. Maybe its yellowed pages hold the answer.

# TWELVE

Mum's sitting on the bench outside the cottage door, lit by the porch lamp. She's still in her dressing gown and she's clutching a full mug of tea in her lap. There's a dark skin across the top of it.

'What you doing out here, Mum?' I say. I take the mug from her hand, tip the contents on to the grass. 'It's getting dark. And the wind's up.'

'Sorry,' she says, her voice bleary, like I've woken her from sleep. 'Must have nodded off.' She fidgets with the collar of her dressing gown. 'I'll get dressed in a minute.' She smiles at me, raises her eyebrows and points at the book under my arm. 'What have you got there?' She puts down her mug, holds out her hands. 'Looks old and interesting.'

I wonder how long she's been sitting here; whether she's bothered to eat or drink anything at all. But she's making an effort to offer me something bright, I can see; something hard for her to find.

I sit beside her and open the book across our laps. 'Just some old book I picked up.'

'What, in the shop?'

'Yep,' I say, not totally sure why I'm lying about it. 'In that crazy shop.'

Mum smooths her hand over a full-page image: a thunderous night sky over a ferocious sea, a sailing ship tilting precariously on black waves, its sails tattered and torn. A weird pasty moon casts a pale shadow to one side of the ship: a ghostly replica of the stricken vessel.

'*The Flying Dutchman*,' Mum reads. '*A legendary Dutch East India Company ship said to have vanished into a storm off the treacherous Cape of Good Hope.*' She bends lower, squints at the faded print on the facing page. Her hair swings forward in stringy strands and she tucks it behind her ears. '*Many have since claimed sightings of the lost ship. According to sailors' folklore, a sighting of a phantom version of the lost clipper is an omen of impending doom . . .*'

We look up, identical expressions of mock-horror on our faces. We laugh, and in that moment she's Mum again. I turn to the next page, try to hold her there with me.

'Wow,' I say, pointing at the looming, bearded face of the Ancient Mariner, his clawed, reaching hands so like those of Meg's grandad in the clifftop storm. 'How cool is that? Looks like he's trying to grab hold of us from the page!'

Mum nods. She runs a finger across the crevices in his face, around one of his peculiar piercing eyes. 'What a face,' she says. 'So many stories. So much fear . . .' Before I can say anything else, she's closed the book. Her eyes are on mine; serious; worried.

'Luke, we need to talk.'

'What about?' I lift the heavy book against my chest, like a shield.

Mum pulls her collar more tightly around her throat, like she's suddenly cold. 'Your guitar,' she says. 'What happened?'

I shrug. 'Who cares?'

She touches my arm. 'You love that guitar, sweetheart. It's part of you.'

I hold her gaze; hold the book closer still.

'*Was* part of me,' I say, studying the fading red grooves on the fingers of my left hand. 'Like lots of things. Like just about every bit of my old life, in case you haven't noticed.' I look away. 'Like Dad.'

Mum reaches round, cups my face in her hands. They're ice cold.

'Luke, is this about that letter? Because whatever it says

93

or doesn't say, your dad is NOT disappearing out of your life. Not while we're here, and not when we go home. He's still your dad. Always *will* be your dad. The new baby won't make any difference to that.'

I push her hands away. 'Yeah, right,' I say. 'So where is he, then?' My words hit the air along with a spray of spit. 'How come he hasn't made sure we're OK, like he promised? How come all he's got for his precious son is a few scribbled words on a scrap of paper?'

I fling the book open again, frantically flip the pages to find the one I want; stab my finger at the image there. 'My so-called "dad" is about as real as this stupid phantom ship.' I slam the book shut. I jump up.

'Luke, sweetheart. Sit down. You're angry; hurt, I know, but –'

'You bet I am,' I shout. 'My dad's opted for some swap-shop family scenario as far away from me as possible, and my mum's not even on the same planet most of the time!'

I leave Mum there, her body sort of collapsed in on itself, like I've punched her; her head bowed like she deserved it too. I thunder up the stairs to my room and fling myself on my bed. I pull the duvet over my head, try to block out the thought that maybe she *does* deserve it. That maybe if she hadn't started hanging round in her

94

dressing gown with unwashed hair, or sleeping all day, Dad would have stayed.

What kind of son thinks like that?

Maybe I'm the one to blame.

For everything.

# THIRTEEN

It's ink-dark when hunger drives me downstairs. Moonlight picks out the splintered remains of my guitar on the kitchen table. Spotlight on a crime scene. There's a bottle of wood glue there too. My heart aches for Mum, who would, I know, mend us all with that hopeless glue, if only she could.

I hate myself all over again.

I make mugs of hot chocolate, grab a packet of cookies, and go to find her. She's curled upon the living-room sofa, staring at the TV screen: some late game show she doesn't like.

I hand her the mug of chocolate. 'Careful, it's hot,' I say, like she's the child I once was. Still am.

She wraps her hands around it, blows on the surface; smiles up at me.

'About earlier,' she says. 'I understand. Really. I do. And I'm sorry, Luke. For being – you know. For not doing better.'

'No,' I say. 'It isn't your fault. Dad. Or any of it. Take no notice. I was being an idiot.' I head back towards the door before she can say anything else – before she can disagree. Or agree. Before she can hear the things I'm not saying. 'I'll get that book again, shall I?' I ask. I don't wait for a reply.

By the time we go to bed I'm something of an expert in seafaring legend and probably far too high on sugar given that I ate the whole packet of cookies but no dinner. But I'm none the wiser about the Otters' Moon.

Somehow, I fall asleep immediately. My dreams are full of sinister shape-shifting seal-humans and the screams of seafaring folk as they search stormy waters for their lost ships, lost loved ones or their stolen souls. Pieces of red Stratocaster mingle with the rolling waves and flailing limbs; disappear from sight. Giant otters leap and play among it all and a vast black moon hangs in the sky like a threat.

Meg doesn't show up until halfway through the next afternoon. And she doesn't come to the door, like a normal person. She appears at the kitchen window, taps on the glass; goes to sit astride the garden gate, legs swinging with what I know will be impatience. Even though *I've* been waiting for *her* for hours. She totally *is* the most annoying person I've ever met.

I grab a bag of provisions that I've had ready since breakfast, add the torch that hangs on the back of the front door for exploring the caves. Once outside the house, I realise that daylight is already fading. I'll need that torch just to find my way home.

'Thought you'd be here earlier,' I say.

'Tide times, remember? I *told* you. And anyway, I thought we could try for another glimpse of the otters. No good going earlier for that.'

'The otters. Great,' I say, trying to sound enthusiastic. 'But what about the caves – hadn't we better go there first? Before the light really goes?'

'Not scared of the dark, are you, city boy?' Meg smirks. It's definitely a smirk.

I shoot her what I hope is a withering look. 'Stop calling me that,' I say, suddenly tired of the put-down behind the name. Like just because I'm not on speaking terms with six species of crab and don't live to hang out with otters, I'm not right somehow. I turn away, follow the drift of a seagull. It lands on the roof of the cottage. Even from here I can tell it's watching me. Even the island birds have a problem with me.

I sigh, turn back to Meg. 'Caves are interesting, that's all,' I say.

'And otters aren't?'

For a moment pushing Meg off the fence seems like a good option.

'Look, I didn't . . . Can we just go?'

She jumps down, retrieves a large rucksack from behind the wall and heaves it on to her shoulder. 'Picnic supper and stuff,' she says. 'I made brownies. And don't worry. No puffin bones this time.' She laughs, shields her vision with one hand against the low-set sun; looks out beyond the cliff edge, towards the sea. When she drops her hand, the sky is reflected in her eyes, blue-grey and streaked with gold.

'Come on, then,' she says. 'Best get going.'

We follow a different route from yesterday, swapping the long scramble across vicious rocks for a (long) fast walk in the other direction: past Meg's house, where smoke curls from the chimney, and along a narrow strip of beach that becomes less sand, more pebbles the further we go. Meg trudges on ahead for a while, more intent on getting where we're going than talking, I guess. Or intent on avoiding talking. There's just the crunch and slide of our steps, the distant roar of the sea; the call of bad-tempered birds. I'm happy with that for now. I don't feel much like talking either. And the sounds soothe the spin of my thoughts: Mum, Dad, the baby intruder all settle somewhere just out of reach. Our shadows move to one side of us, stretch a little taller as we walk; begin to bend and reach up the sides of the cliff face, like they're trying to get away, too.

But my dream – and the old man's moon warning – they stay with me.

I need to know more.

I catch Meg up, match her stride; decide on a gentle approach.

'So, how's your grandad today?'

Seabird eyes again. Narrow, mean ones. 'He's fine,' Meg says. She speeds up a fraction, stumbles as her foot twists among the pebbles. She stops, balances on one leg and unlaces her trainers. 'Much better in bare feet,' she says, looking pointedly at my own shabby footwear.

'I'm good,' I say.

She shrugs. 'Suit yourself. But they'll need to come off up ahead. Unless soggy shoes are your thing. Or dicing with death.'

What was she on about now?

'Look,' I say. 'What's with that boat behind the house?

How come your grandad went all weird when I mentioned it? And this Otters' Moon thing – you going to tell me?'

She opens her mouth to speak.

'Please,' I say, 'I know there's stuff that's hard to talk about, but can you at least answer a couple of simple questions?'

She picks up her shoes, stares down at her feet and wriggles her toes around among the pebbles. 'They're not simple,' she says. 'Your questions. Or the answers. Well, they are, and they're not.'

I blow through my teeth. Wait.

'We need to keep walking,' Meg says. 'But, OK, I'll try, all right?

'That boat,' she says. 'It was Grandad's pride and joy. Best fishing boat he'd ever had. He had a hand in building it too, helped his old shipwright friend, Billy.' She glances at me. 'It was Billy who told me. About – that night.'

I wait. When she speaks again the words tumble out in a rush, like she just untied tethers and set them free from somewhere.

'Grandad took the boat out,' she says. 'On the night Mum and Dad went missing. He shouldn't have – it was way too dangerous by then, but he did. A storm. He was out for hours, searching for Dad. He knew Mum was lost. People told him Dad would be gone too. That it was hopeless in those conditions. The . . . low moonlight. The mist. But he wouldn't listen. How could he? That was his *son*.' Meg takes a breath in, holds it for a second. 'His boat had been snagged on the rocks. He'd somehow managed to make it to Lighthouse Rock. That's where they found him next morning, barely alive in the cold. He blamed himself. For letting Mum – and Dad – go out that night. For not avoiding the rocks. For everything. As soon as he was strong enough again, he hauled that boat up from the harbour and pretty much hurled it down between the dunes there, threw a cover right over it. Never wanted to lay eyes on it again, he told Billy. Never went out in it again; never fished at sea again from that day on.'

'Wow,' I say. 'Poor guy.'

Would my dad do that? I wonder. Put himself at risk to save me? Doubtful. I push the thought away. This isn't about me.

All of a sudden, the air feels colder; damp. Not sea-spray damp. Something more. I pull my sweatshirt from my bag and put it on. Give Meg some space.

'So, your grandad never got over it, losing your dad?' I say. 'And your mum. That's what makes him –' I search for the words – 'you know, muddled, sometimes?'

'Yes. No. Not exactly. Like I said, it's complicated.' The

searing blue stare again. 'Look, if I tell you, you can't say a word. Not to Grandad, and NEVER to anyone else.'

More secrets: the otters all over again. But this time those seabird eyes are different: it looks like the seawater is in them, threatening to spill over on to Meg's cheeks. She stands still, shakes her head.

'He was fine before. I mean, he cried, loads. But he coped. For my sake. He said Mum and Dad were still with us – you know, everywhere around us. In the plants; the flowers, the sea creatures. Everything. He's got this theory . . . about us all being connected; all part of the natural world around us.' She waves her hand. 'He was brilliant. Is brilliant. He tried to make up for things. We had fun. He taught me stuff.'

A strand of hair blows across her mouth. She draws it in, chews at it; spits it out.

'Something's wrong, Luke,' she says. 'Something's changed. Sometimes he's still just Grandad, but then, other times, he's like . . . this little lost boy; scared and confused – just not *with* me. And more and more, he's back there, that night, like it's happening right then. Like he's got to go and find Mum and Dad all over again.' A single fat tear escapes and runs down the side of Meg's nose. She bats it away, speaks her next words into the air. 'Sometimes,' she whispers, 'he thinks *I'm* Mum.'

I nod. Even though Meg can't see me.

That day, on the cliff top. I was David. His son. He was trying to save me.

I think of Mum, how I wish I could reach her; save her from this dark thing inside her.

Of Dad, how I wish he'd come back and save us both.

A fist squeezes around my heart.

Meg is still talking.

'Lately, Grandad gets obsessed with stuff. The island weather. Phases of the moon.' She pauses, looks at me. 'The boarded-up windows . . .'

Another nod.

'That's to stop Grandad watching the whole time. For signs. Warnings, he calls them.'

'What warnings?'

Meg shrugs; shakes her head. 'Some mist – something he thinks might get in through the windows at night . . . I don't know. Doesn't make much sense.' She smiles; a soft smile that I feel in the middle of me. 'Like I said, he's a great one for stories. Always was. Guess they've sort of got mixed in with real stuff. With the sad stuff.'

'Can't someone help him?' I say. 'I mean, a doctor or someone?'

'No.' Meg spins round to face me. 'No doctors. They'll put him in a home. Like they did with his friend Billy. Billy coped, quite liked the company, I think. But Grandad wouldn't survive a move like that. The island's his life, all he's ever known . . .' She looks at her feet again. 'They'd put me in a home, too.'

'Isn't there, you know, someone else? Other family or something?'

'*I'm* Grandad's family,' she says, her words like a whiplash. 'And he's mine.'

'Right,' I say. 'I just thought, I mean –'

'Forget about it, OK?' Meg grabs my arm. 'Grandad and me, we'll be fine. Like always.'

She falls silent. I pick my way along behind her, someone else's worries heavy in my chest for once, instead of my own. At least I still have Mum in my corner, even if she's can't see me at times. And Dad's out there. Even if he doesn't remember me. But Meg: how long before she's totally alone in the world? I stare at her slumped shoulders and I'm silent, too.

In the sound-space that's left, there's something new. A deep surging rumble that becomes louder as we walk.

It's water. Lots of water. Close by.

Very close.

'You did check the tide times?' I say, trying to disguise the pinch of fear in my voice.

Meg shoots me a derisory glance. She's back, at least.

I scan the area for means of escape. There's none. The cliff face here is sheer and in the other direction there's only the sea. The pebbled beach is growing darker, slick with water, even though the tide is well out. Allegedly. Large chunks of mossy rock are strewn across the pebbled beach, as if lobbed through the air by a giant. Pools of water lie cradled between them.

Meg points up ahead, round another deep curve in the bay. 'You'll see in a minute.' She grins. 'Time to get those trainers off, city boy.'

I let the name go.

# FOURTEEN

We clamber over slippery boulders. And Meg's right. It's easier in bare feet. Except when you have a pair of shoes under one arm and a bag bouncing on your back.

Meg sits on a rock and ties her trainers together, loops the laces around her neck. I try to do the same. Even that's not easy with cold wet fingers and Meg is hopping from one foot to the other like an impatient bird by the time I'm done. I ignore her; roll my jeans up too. I think suddenly of my own grandad that last summer, trousers up over his spindly calves: knotted handkerchief on his head as he snoozed in his garden chair. I wonder about the stories *he* had to tell; wish I'd thought to ask.

And just for a moment I wonder whether there's more to Meg's grandad's worries than she's letting on. They're both full of secrets. What if there's some truth in those warnings of his? What if I'm in some kind of danger on Mum's supposed island sanctuary?

Maybe I should tell someone. Dad. (If I could get hold of him.)

No point, I decide. 'Tall tales,' he'd say. 'Just the wanderings of old age,' he'd say.

And he'd be right. Of course he would.

I need to get a grip.

As we begin to skirt the curve of the bay, the cliff face alongside us becomes more rugged and coated in vivid green moss. Curled feathery ferns and something that might be honeysuckle sprout from cracks there. Trees protrude at impossible angles, like they might be levitating in the air. The rock-and-pebble beach is broken up with patches of sandy grass. The rock pools are larger.

The watery surge is like thunder now; the salt sting of the sea air mingles with something that reminds me of damp forest floors, or our garden after rain.

Meg turns and says something I can't hear.

She tries again.

I shake my head, shrug; hope it wasn't anything important. She sets off again and is soon well ahead, footsure as ever. I stumble, bang my knee; inspect it for damage. No blood. When I look up, Meg's disappeared round a sharp dog-leg bend in the cliff face. I scramble after her.

There's a waterfall.

No. Three waterfalls.

Narrow tumbling torrents of crystal-clear water cascade down the cliff face, crash and foam over green velvet-coated rocks at their base; bounce over stones and pebbles and run in silver ribbons into the distance. Sunlight glances off them, creating fleeting rainbow prisms.

Meg is standing stock-still, hands on hips, head thrown back. Her hair floats and twists like seaweed in the damp air. Her eyes are tightly closed. I join her, close mine too; listen to the roar of the water. Spray lands like a cool net on my skin.

Meg nudges my arm, leans in as I open my eyes; cups her hand around my ear.

'Impressed, city boy?' she shouts. 'Just think, this waterfall, these rocks: here – the same – for millions of years. Think what they've seen: dinosaurs, Bronze Age man, Vikings . . .'

I stare upwards; imagine pterodactyls soaring above, apatosaurs stretching their long necks to tear the ferns from the cliff face. I see primeval spears and primitive tools among the rocks and stones. Something builds in my chest, like the surge and beauty of the waterfall is in there too. I feel impossibly small.

'Impressed,' I whisper. And I smile.

'A first for you, that,' Meg shouts into my ear.

I'm back down to earth. Where does she think I've been? 'I *have* seen waterfalls before,' I say. 'Just not – all of this . . .'

'The smile. I meant the smile.' Meg skips out of my reach, her bubble of a laugh lost to the waterfalls.

I smile again. Because she has a point. Because the stretch of my own smile feels good – forgotten. Surprising.

Because I like her laugh.

She beckons to me, points downwards towards the foot of the first of them.

I push strands of dripping hair from my forehead and follow her gaze.

'Caves,' she mouths.

Or I think she does. I see only a kind of dark fold in the rock face. Before I can reply, she's climbing down towards it – finding handholds and footholds as if by instinct. She's been this way before.

Not so easy for me.

I manage a slow shuffle-and-crawl combo. My feet keep slipping. I try not to look down too far, and only know that I've made it to the supposed cave when I hear an excited *whoop*. Meg's voice for sure, but strangely hollow.

Her face follows; disappears again behind a swinging fern curtain.

I push through the feathered fronds.

'Ta-da!' Meg spreads her arms wide, twirls around like an overexcited tour guide.

Late low sunlight flickers through the leafy door, reveals a kind of round antechamber that narrows then stretches dimly ahead.

I look up. The ceiling here is vaulted, like a cathedral or something; the vast walls ridged blue and grey like the pipes of an enormous church organ in places. The rumble of the water outside is punctuated by a deep echoing drip somewhere *in*side. A kind of underground musical intro . . .

'Awesome,' is all I can manage. Because *really* awesome is much too big for words.

Meg grins. 'Amazing, right?' Her face shines in the dancing light.

I nod, move further inside; stretch out a hand, run it over the wall nearest to me. It's cold; smooth in places, sharp in others. I remember the torch in my – now sodden – backpack, and pull it out, hope there isn't too much water inside it.

Meg pushes further ahead. 'Look,' she calls, directing

the yellow beam just above her head. Her voice echoes, bounces around the cave.

'Wow,' I say. I swing my own torchlight in an arc. 'Wow.'

Thousands of tiny shells are embedded in the walls and ceiling. In places curled feather-like imprints, fern 'fossils', are captured in the rock. It's like someone decorated in here; made mosaics. And there's this sense of stepping back in time: of ancient lives frozen all around us.

For once I'm as excited as Meg.

'See the black smudges there?' she says. 'Smoke from settlers' fires. Centuries of them. Found some of my best bones and skulls here: animals and birds – things that went in the cooking pot; things that crawled in here to die.'

'Right,' I say. I see fur-clad figures hunched around a glowing fire, chewing and spitting out bones. Hopefully, none of them came from humans. I shiver.

'What's up there?' I say, lighting up the narrowing tunnel ahead. 'Have you been that far too? Is there room to explore?'

Meg nods. 'Course I have,' she says.

'Silly question,' I mutter. 'So, come on, then . . .' I turn my torch to full beam, hoist my bag back on to my shoulder.

'You won't need that for long.' Meg stuffs her own torch back into her bag.

She laughs. 'You'll see,' she says. 'And I don't know about you, but I'm starving, so follow me. I'll show you a great place for a picnic.'

The ceiling lowers quickly as we move further inside the cave. We have to drop to our hands and knees. I tug at Meg's bare foot as it threatens to be swallowed up round a sudden bend.

'Wait,' I breathe. 'I'm not sure . . . How much further till it opens out again?'

The foot vanishes, leaving me no option but to follow.

I crawl after it, just as my torch battery flickers, fades, dies.

I'm inside a stone corridor, one that presses in on me from all sides. I have the sense that I'm crawling upwards. Where to, I have no idea. I can't see Meg.

My heart hammers; an echoing drumbeat in my head.

'Meg,' I call. 'Meg! Hang on.' My voice ricochets around me, comes back at me. It sounds scared. There's nothing from Meg.

# FIFTEEN

I have no choice but to keep going. I crawl forward, fight my rising panic. It's only seconds since I saw Meg. No doubt she'll pop up round the next bend with that smug smile of hers. Well, I'm not going to give her the satisfaction of thinking her little disappearing trick has got to me. I take a deep breath; speed up.

There's light coming from somewhere now, the brush of cool air on my face and a definite scrabbling sound that I can only hope is being made by Meg. I stop, find I can kneel up here. I look around, searching for the source of the fresh air.

The tunnel divides – I can either go left, where the ceiling seems to drop even lower, or straight ahead. I call Meg's name again.

A whistle comes from the left fork. Or at least I think it does.

Then that laugh-bubble again. 'Up here, city boy!'

I inch forward.

Just a few paces along the left-hand fork, light pools on the dusty floor. Meg's face appears from above, upside down, her yellow hair swinging underneath it.

'C'mon,' she calls. 'It's easy.' And she's gone.

Right now, pulling that hair hard – pulling *her* back down to join me – feels like a great idea. Does she enjoy making me feel stupid?

I wriggle along into the spotlight; look upwards. Just above head height, I see sky.

Meg's face pops back through the hole. 'Picnic's up,' she says. 'Quick, before I demolish the brownies.' She feeds a thick coil of rope down towards me. 'You sort of abseil,' she shouts. 'Easy toeholds to help you.'

I examine the rope. It's frayed, grubby; ancient. I'm betting it came from the back of that time-slip shop. I grasp it between both hands, pray that it's stronger than it looks and that it's properly secured. I pull my trainers back on, stick one foot into a hole in the cave wall and lift myself from the ground.

My foot slips out. I spin on the rope for a moment, step down. I try again. I don't exactly have an option.

My palms burn as I heave myself upwards; swinging alarmingly from side to side in my search for the 'easy toeholds'. I'm probably at the top within

115

two minutes, but it feels like two years.

I tell myself this is the last time I follow Meg anywhere at all. It won't be. I know that. She's weird and infuriating but she's the only thing between me and death by boredom.

She's the only one with the answers . . .

She's sitting cross-legged on a blue blanket, surrounded by paper plates piled with rough-cut sandwiches, bright red apples and slightly squashed chocolate brownies. By the look of her chin she's already eaten one of those. She holds out a carton of juice.

'Looks like you could use this,' she says. With that grin of hers.

'No, thanks.' I throw my bag out first, then clamber out on to springy moss 'Got my own.' I gulp fresh air into my lungs.

Meg reaches for a sandwich, waves it in my direction. 'What's up? Too tough down there for a city boy?'

'Not tough. Annoying,' I say, and swig from my water bottle. 'You, that is. You and your stupid disappearing trick. You always trying to show me up – the whole "stupid city-kid" thing.'

I wipe sweat from my eyes. I look around me. But I'm seeing another landscape. Another life. Me, mud-sliding between goalposts, a ball in the back of the net. Yells and screams of victory. The thud of Jez and Luca or daft Slogger landing on my back.

The feeling that I'm the best.

That I belong.

'I'm sorry,' Meg says.

I blink, jump back into now.

'I don't – I didn't mean –' Meg gestures at the spread of food – swings her arms wide. 'I wanted to surprise you,' she says, her voice softer, like maybe she really did. 'The food. The tunnels. This place . . .'

I don't hear any more. I'm staring around. My mouth really does drop open.

This place. I have to admit: it's fantastic.

We're on a rocky plateau. It overhangs low grassy dunes. Beyond them a satin-flat river coils around an expanse of green, dwindles towards a strip of sand and on towards the sea. I can just make out the flick of white frothy waves on the shoreline. Partway out – close enough to paddle, I'm guessing – two huge tall stones reach into the sky from a miniature stone island. Their reflections reach towards the land: wavering black fingers on the surface of the water.

'Standing stones,' Meg says. 'Dated to Neolithic times, or earlier. Cool, aren't they?'

I nod. 'This whole place is cool,' I say, my frustration

with Meg, my missing my mates, swept to one side by the surprising beauty of it all. The history that hangs in the air.

My stomach growls. I brush sand from my hands, reach for a brownie. 'Why are they there?' I ask, between sticky mouthfuls. 'Those stones. Do they, you know, *mean* something?'

'No one's sure,' Meg says. 'Maybe something to do with the sun – worship or whatever. Some people say they were a sort of marker – a boundary.' She looks away into the distance. 'Or a warning, maybe.'

'What kind of warning?'

She shrugs. 'Who knows? There are stories – all a bit confused. Hard to sort fact from fiction on an ancient island like this.'

No kidding.

Meg drains her carton of juice, presses it flat and shoves it down inside her bag.

'There are others dotted around the island,' she says. 'Only on this side, though.'

'Can you show me?' I say, surprised by my own question. I pretty much yawned my way through a school trip to Stonehenge last year. But this side of the island – the scenery, the stories – they've got my attention.

'There are some where the otters hang out. We're going

back that way.' She hands me the plate of sandwiches. 'Eat. I've got to be back home before it's dark.'

'Not scared, are you, island girl?'

'Funny,' she says. But this time her grin is wide; warmer.

I swallow a bite of sandwich. They're egg and cress, which I hate. But they taste different today. Better, out here in the salt air.

'I can eat as we go,' I say. 'Unless there's more caving involved.'

She shakes her head. Wipes her fingers on her dungarees. 'No. Overland walk this time. That way.' She points down to the beach.

'Good,' I say.

'Thought you liked caves.' Meg laughs. 'You wouldn't have made a smuggler.'

'Smuggler?'

Meg nods. 'Smugglers used those caves as well as settlers. They probably widened some of the tunnels too. And chipped out the footholds we used to climb.' She waits for a response.

I raise my eyebrows. It's in her genes to spin stories. I'm still deciding whether I like that about her.

'Historical fact,' Meg says, beginning to pack up.

I snatch an apple and a second brownie before they

disappear, stuff them in my pocket.

'Late 1700s it was, mainly. They brought in barrels of brandy, rum or tobacco from abroad. Or took Scottish whisky out of the country to sell at a huge profit. That was against the law. And food was smuggled in *and* out at times: corn and stuff like that. People were hungry.'

'Wow.' I picture furtive men, barrels and sacks shouldered high; small boats bobbing in the late-night bay. 'Was there trouble?'

Meg nods. 'Lots of trouble. Tussles with islanders – fights with the king's men . . .'

'Redcoats?' I say, fragments of a film watched with Dad suddenly in my head. The memory belongs to another life. Another me. I get to my feet, peer down at the bay.

'Redcoats, among others,' Meg says. 'There were some bloody battles on this beach.' She scoops up the blanket, shakes it; rolls it into a tight sausage and squashes it into her bag. 'That's if the sea didn't take the smugglers first,' she adds. 'They had to dock their ships well out and row in under cover of darkness. Flimsy boats. Rocks. Things . . . like I said . . .'

She stops, turns away.

I remember why.

We're both still for a moment.

'Grandad loved this place when he was a boy,' she says. 'He and Billy, they used to make dens in those caves; hide down there when they were supposed to be at school.'

'What's his name – your grandad?' I ask. 'His first name, I mean.'

'Seth.' Meg smiles. 'Like his father and grandfather before him. Little tearaway, he was. Up to all sorts, according to Billy.'

I try to picture that young Seth. Wild, wind-blown. Fearless.

I think I've glimpsed him, seen him peering out from behind the old man's watery blue stare.

'Sun's almost setting,' Meg says. She hands me my backpack. 'But don't think you're escaping some quick litter duty.'

'As if,' I say. Although I was hoping I had.

'By the time we're done it'll be otter playtime again. If you're lucky.' Meg's seabird eyes are back, fixed on mine. 'And if you do exactly what I tell you when we get near their bit of the bay. OK?'

I sling my bag over one shoulder. 'What's new?' I say. My turn to grin.

I pick up a flat grey pebble, weigh it in my hand; wonder whether once, long ago, a blue-eyed boy – or a reckless smuggler – did what I was about to do next.

I throw the pebble into the air; send it skipping off the rocks, down towards the silent stone sea giants that know the answer.

# SIXTEEEN

We wait silently for the otter family to appear, hunched low behind the turtle-shell boat. I'm tired, happy to be still for a while. I watch for the quiver of a whiskered nose in the seagrass. For a rolling ball of limbs, tails and black-bead eyes to burst from behind rocks. I wonder about the pups' mother; how big she'll be. Whether she'll sense our presence and hurry her babies away to safety. That's what mothers do.

I'm surprised by my disappointment when there's nothing.

The sun does the sudden disappearing trick that still catches me unawares here. We're plunged into a murky moonlight. It makes me uneasy. I think of Mum, still by herself at the cottage, hope she hasn't sunk too far into her own low-lit world without me there to distract her.

I nudge Meg; shrug. 'Shouldn't we get going?' I whisper.

Maybe Meg is worrying, too. She kneels up, scans the bay one last time.

'OK,' she says. 'Never mind. We can come back tomorrow.' She looks at me. 'See you at your gate. Around ten? If you want.'

I nod. 'Should be OK,' I say.'

Maybe the island – and its wild inhabitants – are growing on me.

We'll see.

A stream of deep yellow light shines into the darkness from the boathouse doorway, stretches towards us as we round the cliff towards Meg's bay.

Meg shoves her bag at me, speeds towards the house.

'Grandad,' she shouts. 'Grandad.' She slips inside, reappears seconds later, flashlight in hand. 'He's not here! Grandad!' she yells. 'It's Meg. I'm back. Where are you?'

A shadowy figure stumbles out from the dunes as just as I reach Meg.

'You were gone,' the old man says, his voice pitched high, his pale face ghostly in the swing of the flashlight. 'You were gone, Catherine.'

Meg puts her arm round his shoulders, gestures for me to back off with the other.

'I'm sorry,' she says. 'I'm here now. Let's get you inside.'

She doesn't look back. The boathouse door closes with a snap.

The night around me turns velvet black, as if the moon has been swallowed up inside, along with Meg and Seth. Not a sliver of light escapes from the boarded-up windows. I think of the fear behind the blinded panes. Wonder again how much of it is real outside of Seth's closing-down mind. Probably not much. Reassuring, I suppose. But sad.

Sand spirals: a small, spiteful whirlwind that sweeps away my good feelings about the day. It feels deliberate. The cry of a single bird lifts above it, shrill; scared. My heartbeat sounds in my ears for the second time today: deep and echoing; notes from a bass guitar.

I need to get home.

I throw Meg's bag on the doorstep, ferret about in mine for my torch. It's dead. Of course it is. Nothing left to see me up the steep cliff path to the cottage.

I feel my way along much of it, senses sharpened by anxiety. I manage to make it in record time.

The kitchen is warm and smells of food: Mum's been cooking. Something spicy and sweet. My favourite korma curry for sure. The table is set – plates, cutlery, glasses. She's made a real effort.

I glance at the clock: eight thirty. Even later than I thought. Too late.

Mum's trying and I've ruined it all.

She's on the sofa in the lounge, laptop on her knee. She shoves it aside and gets to her feet. She's dressed. Her face is less pale, like she might have spent some time outside today; found some sunlight.

'Luke,' she says, eyes scanning me for answers. Or imagined injuries. 'It's so late . . .' Her shoulders sink with relief.

'I know,' I say. 'I'm really sorry, Mum. I lost track of time.'

She smiles a watery smile. 'You were having fun, then? This "boring island" not so bad after all?'

I smile back, nod. 'Maybe,' I say. I'd feel better if she got angry. Want her to be.

Instead, she reaches for me, wraps her arms around me for a moment. Which is better. It's a while since she's done that. But she feels fragile, all bones. She *has* to eat more.

Maybe her cooking today is a breakthrough: the island working some magic like she said it would.

'You made dinner,' I say. 'Chicken korma?'

Mum nods. 'Your favourite. Might be a bit dry by now.'

'Thanks, Mum. Smells amazing,' I say. 'Let's go.'

It feels good sitting across the table from Mum in the warm kitchen, eating together. Almost like old times. Although I'm the one doing most of the eating.

I itch to tell her about Puffin Bay, the caves. The otters. Anything that might catch her interest; might hold her here so she doesn't slip away from me again. I think of the small acrobats tussling in the water; unafraid. Free. I remember Meg's seabird stare.

I could tell her about Meg and her grandad, at least. But I don't. I'm not sure why. Maybe I just want them for myself; something separate from the broken bits of my home life. Or maybe I'm afraid the old man's warnings – his fear, the fear *I* can't quite shake – might leak through. Mum doesn't need more things to worry about.

'Chicken's amazing,' I say. I scrape up the last traces of sauce.

Mum winces at the screech of my fork on the china plate.

'I'm glad. I wanted it to be special.' She takes the serving dish to the sink, plugs in the kettle, sits down again. 'There's some news, Luke.' She covers my hand with hers. 'Some lovely news.'

'Dad's coming?' The words sound hollow, even as they come out of my mouth. I hate myself for hoping.

Mum shakes her head. 'No, but he emailed this morning. Both of us.'

I look round for my laptop, remember I left it on my bed, needing to charge. I watch Mum's face.

'Jenny's baby's here, Luke.' She lifts a smile on to her face. I can feel the effort it takes from across the table. 'You have a sister.'

Steam billows from the kettle. The automatic switch kicks in, loud in the silent room.

The steam is in my head too, building.

I shove my chair back. It screeches against the flagstone floor.

'She's not my sister,' I hiss. 'She's nothing to do with me.'

'Luke, sweetheart, sit down. Please.'

'Fat chance of ever seeing Dad now.' I thump the table. The plates shudder. My knife and fork leap in the air, clatter back down again. 'Not now he's got *her*.'

'I know this is hard, Luke. I do. For both of us. But this baby, she's your sister. Half-sister, anyway.' Her voice is thin, strained. 'Although, I don't think anyone is "half anything". Not really. She's your dad's child, just like you. And none of this . . . trouble is her fault.'

'No,' I shout, 'we all know who's to blame for that. For *her*.'

128

'Read your dad's message. He can't wait to introduce the baby to her big brother. He'll make it happen very soon. He promises.'

'No way.' I snatch up the dirty plates, slam them into the sink and turn on the tap. Mum's uneaten curry slides into the bowl, turning the water to the colour of old blood.

'Let's talk this out, sweetheart,' Mum says.

'Nothing to say.' I reach for the knives and forks, throw them into the dark swirling water, watch it drain away. There's a jagged crack across the middle of my green plate. It splits into two parts as I lift it from the bowl. 'Words can't mend things.'

She stares at me. 'They can,' she says, her voice changing key. Like it's a question. Or a wish. 'They might.'

'Thanks again for dinner, Mum,' I say. 'I'm shattered. I'm going to bed.'

I hear her sigh as I reach the door, look back. She's crumpled in on herself like a deflated balloon.

*Nice one, Dad.*

*Nice one, Luke.*

The night is eerily still outside my window, the moon especially bright. I don't sleep. I lie there, listening for the sound of Mum crying in the next room. Dreading it.

It doesn't come. Which is even worse. Sometimes I

think she's turning to stone from the inside, like some stupid fairy-tale curse has imprisoned her.

I'm part of the curse. I know I am.

I'm the spitting image of Dad. Everyone says so. His whole international family mix is right there, like a map of the world picked out in skin, bone and hair. No trace of Mum. She used to joke about it; how unfair it was, when she did all the hard work growing me.

I was 'a chip off the old block', Grandpa said. He used to be so proud of that.

So did I.

But every time Mum looks at me, she sees *him*. No wonder she can't forget, can't recover, with me around.

What about the shiny new child? Is she like Dad too?

Like me?

No doubt the proud father sent a photo of her with his email.

The moon pushes through my thin curtains, glances off the silver lid of my laptop. Taunts me. I crawl out of bed and shove the laptop – and my so-called sister – under the bed. As far as I can reach. Dust catches in my throat.

I go to the bathroom for a glass of water, treading softly past Mum's door on the ancient wooden floorboards. Still no sound from her room.

On the shelf above the loo there's a plastic bottle minus its lid. A few golden droplets cling to its white neck.

Mum's new healthy glow. That's not real either.

I go back to bed and pull the covers over my head.

When I emerge, I'm squinting in the brightness of the day. My mouth is bone dry. There's a boulder in my stomach. It's several seconds before I remember who put it there.

I wonder about the time. Whether Mum is still in bed too. I should check.

I can't be bothered to move.

The door creaks open. Mum's face appears, her hair wild, stringy, like the windblown seagrass on the cliffs.

'You OK, sweetheart?' she says, moving into the room. 'Only it's gone twelve o'clock. Do you want breakfast? Brunch. We could have pancakes again . . .'

I shake my head. 'No, thanks,' I say. 'Not feeling too good.'

Mum sits on the end of the bed, pushes strands of hair from my eyes, presses her palm on my forehead. Memories flicker: fevers and childish furies soothed away with a touch. A smile. A shiny coin to spend on pick-and-mix in the corner shop.

Heat builds behind my eyes. I jerk my head away.

'No temperature,' Mum says. 'You might feel better if you get up, have something to eat.'

'No thanks. I'll have some water.' I reach for the glass on my bedside cabinet.

Mum gets up, draws her dressing gown tightly around her. I remember last night's bird-bone hug.

'Those pancakes,' I say. 'Make them for yourself. I expect I'll want some later too.'

Mum nods. 'OK.'

She turns back as she gets to the door.

'Luke, about . . . the baby – we *can* talk. You don't need to protect me.'

I wriggle further under the duvet. 'It's not that,' I say. 'I told you, I'm sickening for something.'

'Rest, then. Try and sleep it off,' Mum says.

She's not fooled. I know that. She just doesn't have the energy for the truth.

Neither do I.

But it's here, anyway. Staring through the face of a newborn girl.

Dad is NOT coming back.

His 'happy news' has kicked a huge hole right through the middle of me. A hope-shaped hole I didn't know was there.

Before I drift off again, I remember about Meg. How long did she wait at the gate?

She'll be furious. But she didn't come knocking, at least. She wouldn't.

For once I'm grateful for weird, secretive ways.

# SEVENTEEN

It's dark again when a tap at the kitchen window proves me wrong.

Meg's face looms between the partly drawn curtains, her eyes wide and urgent. I'm halfway through a cold pancake. On my own. I'm not in the mood for one of Meg's lectures. Not in the mood for talking.

She taps again, louder this time. Beckons to me.

She'll disturb Mum, who's only just stopped pacing and nodded off in the lounge. I glance at the clock. Eight o'clock. Really?

I hold my finger to my lips, go to the front door, open it just a crack.

'I'm sick,' I hiss. 'Probably infectious.'

'You look fine. Come outside a minute.'

'Can't. Got a fever.'

'Fresh air's good for fever. Grandad always –'

The lounge floorboards creak. Mum's on the move again.

I glance over my shoulder, slide the latch on the front

134

door and slip outside. Cool air lifts the hairs on my arms. I shiver. There's a strong smell of fish again. I'm pretty sure it's coming from Meg.

'You can still walk, then?' she says.

I tug at her sleeve, move her further way from the house.

'You've woken my mum now,' I whisper. 'Just go home, OK? You can have a go at me tomorrow. Something for you to look forward to.'

'Shut up, Luke. I've only got a minute.' Meg's eyes flash in the darkness. 'I need your help. Tomorrow. Early. It's the otters.'

I sigh. There's no room in my head for Meg *or* her otter emergency. Right now, I don't even know how to help myself.

'I told you, I'm sick.'

'You'll be better by then,' Meg says. 'I know you will.'

'Tea leaves told you that, did they?'

A top-floor window lights up behind us, throwing yellow squares on the grass beside us. The bathroom. Or is it my bedroom?

I should get inside.

'OK. All right,' I whisper. 'Ten o'clock at the steps?'

Meg shakes her head. 'Nine. Sharp. And *be* there this time. It's urgent.'

She turns on her heel, crunches way too loudly down the garden path. She climbs over the gate, stops. 'Bring money,' she calls. 'And not a word to your mum about why.'

I slip inside just as Mum appears in the hall.

'Just getting some fresh air,' I say, annoyed at myself for being sucked into Meg's subterfuge. Although I must admit, I'm intrigued. About the money, anyway.

'Feeling a bit better?' Mum says. 'Did you eat?'

'Did you?'

'I made soup.'

She didn't. Unless she made it from non-existent ingredients. The cupboards were pretty bare last time I looked.

Mum runs her hand through her hair. 'Don't be worrying about me, Luke. I'm fine. A bit tired, that's all. I'll head back to bed, I think.' She comes close, looks into my face. 'Unless you feel like talking?'

I shake my head. 'I'm going back up too,' I say.

I watch her climb the stairs, feet slow and heavy. I think that if she believed in her own wise words and shared her feelings with someone – anyone – maybe she'd feel a little lighter.

Maybe then, I *could* let her carry a few of mine.

I'm at the clifftop steps by a quarter to nine, five pounds of my birthday money in my jeans pocket. Wind throws gritty sand in my face. Meg doesn't arrive until twenty past. She's red-faced, out of breath and carrying some kind of box draped in heavy yellow cloth. Oilskin, I think.

'Sorry,' she says. 'Grandad. Did you remember cash? How much have you got?'

'*Hi, Luke,*' I say. I spit sand from my tongue. '*Thanks for coming. Glad you're feeling better. Let me tell you what's going on.*'

Meg plonks the box down on the sand. Gives me another of her bird stares. She has quite a repertoire.

'Fine. But can we just get going first?'

'No way. I'm not up for tagging along on another of your mystery tours. Spill. Starting with that . . . box thing. What is it?'

Meg sighs, pulls back part of the oilskin.

It's a large cage. Thick wire mesh, with a sort of metal plate at the top and a solid base.

'Humane cat trap,' Meg announces, as if that explains everything. 'Watch.' She fiddles with the top of the cage, and the metal plate swings down with a snap, dividing the inside space in two.

I stare at her. I wouldn't have thought traps were her thing, *humane* or otherwise. And cats? Where do they come into it?

'So, don't tell me: you found giant otter-eating cats on the island?'

She readjusts the trap, covers it.

'There are, actually,' she says. 'Wild cats. Lynx-like. Fearsome creatures.'

'Right,' I say. 'And dinosaurs.'

Meg glares. 'You'll know when you meet one. Twice the size of your city cats; two hundred times fiercer.'

'Seen one, have you?'

Meg shakes her head. 'There aren't too many left these days. But there are a few. Hiding out. In the caves. They sneak out to meet with the village moggies, though. Check out the cats you do see around the island. Lots of them are domestic wildcat hybrids: long legs, pointy ears, extra-long ringed tails. Bright emerald eyes that look right through you. Dead giveaway.'

'In the caves,' I say. 'Right. Terrifying.'

Another story. Otherwise she'd have mentioned them yesterday. Wouldn't she?

Meg shrugs. 'We need to get to the shop,' she says.

'Help me carry this thing. I'll tell you what we're doing on the way.'

The trap is heavy, even between the two of us. It bangs against my shins as we climb the cliff staircase to the shop.

'Keep in step,' Meg says. 'That's the trick.'

'Slow down,' I hiss. '*That's* the trick, I think you'll find.'

She doesn't. And neither does the wind. When we reach the top of the steps, it does its best to blow us back down again.

The shop isn't open yet. Maybe the shopkeeper is off delivering another letter. If so, I hope it isn't for me.

Fierce metal grids shield the windows. No chance of a night-time smash-and-grab raid for Tom Piper tinned steak, then.

I lean against the wall. 'So?' I say. '*What's* so urgent with the otters?'

Meg's brow creases with worry. 'It's the otter mum,' she says, her voice husky. 'Something's happened to her. Yesterday, when I was rubbish clearing – on my own – there was –' She falters. Bites her lip. 'There was an otter. An adult. Caught up in some netting – like the stuff we found, remember?'

I nod.

'It was her.' Meg sits on top of the trap. Looks at her

feet. 'The mum. Same white spot on her nose, same bit missing from her tail. She must have swum into it when she was hunting.'

I imagine the helpless creature struggling for freedom; her babies dancing on the shoreline, unaware. 'Sorry,' I say, regretting my sarcastic tone. 'That's horrible.'

'I should have done a better job, been down there every day, not playing tour guide to a city boy who doesn't even know what an otter looks like.'

My fault. It would be. I bite my tongue.

'So, what?' I point at the trap. 'We're taking her to the vet?'

Even this place has a vet, surely.

Meg looks up. The sky trembles in her wide, watery stare. 'She didn't make it,' she says. 'I was too late.'

I don't know what to say.

'Nature's way, I suppose,' I manage. Something my dad says. As if that makes bad things fair.

I think of the motherless otter babies; try to make the words fit. They don't.

But then, fair doesn't seem very important. Not anywhere.

The rattle of window shutters saves me from my thoughts. They fly upwards and judder to a halt. There's the sound of heavy bolts being drawn back. The shopkeeper's shiny head appears around the door. He grimaces, as if customers are the last thing he wants to find. He dodges back inside.

'So what *is* the trap for then?'

Meg shrugs. 'Just in case, that's all.' She jumps to her feet. 'Got the money?'

'Fiver,' I say. 'What's *that* for?'

'The orphans,' she says. 'And we need to be quick.'

# EIGHTEEN

None the wiser about what we're buying – or how exactly Meg thinks we can help wild baby otters – I follow her into the dim interior of the shop. She drops six tins of sardines into a basket. She hurries to the ancient freezer. Her torso vanishes inside as she ferrets around. She adds two packs of what might be frozen eels to the basket, moves aside greying fillets of 'fresh' fish in the chiller and finds a large piece of pink salmon. She seems oblivious to the scrutiny of the shopkeeper, but I feel his button eyes boring into my back the whole time.

I get it now. We're buying otter food. According to the copperplate writing on the price tags, young otters have expensive tastes.

I nudge Meg's arm. 'You *have* got money too?' I say, in the hushed whisper this shop seems to demand. 'Only there's more than a fiver's worth in that basket.'

She tuts, dives between the shelves and plonks herself at the counter.

The shopkeeper's puppet-like features shift. He smiles a stiff smile, reveals a row of perfect, polished teeth. 'Meghan,' he says. 'How's your grandfather? Well, I trust?' He speaks slowly, his lilting Scottish syllables carefully articulated, as if he doesn't use them very often, so has to think hard about each one.

Meg smiles back. 'He's wonderful, thank you, Mr Campbell. Just a wee bit stiff in his legs. That war wound playing up. You'll know fine well about that yourself. I'll tell him you were asking about him, will I?'

A war wound? First I've heard.

Mr Campbell's smile widens. He nods. 'Aye, lassie. Do.'

He points at the basket. 'Anything else for ye, Meghan?'

She tilts her head to one side, looking for all the world like one of the birds she loves so much. 'You wouldn't happen to have some kitten milk going spare? Only we found this family of feral cats: mum and babies. Living under Grandad's old boat. Half-starved, poor wee mites.'

She must sense my open-mouthed stare because she steps on my foot. Hard.

Mr Campbell taps the side of his nose with a manicured finger. He moves aside a dusty velvet door curtain behind him and slips through the gap.

Meg pulls a battered green purse from the pocket of

her dungarees, takes out a fiver and a couple of two-pound coins. She looks up at me.

'What?' she says.

I shake my head, more convinced than ever that I've entered a parallel universe.

Mr Campbell reappears, closes the curtains behind him. He hands Meg a large can, its label faded and peeling away in places. He slides one hand inside his jacket and, with a theatrical flourish, produces a small flat box.

'For the fleas,' he announces.

'Wonderful, thank you,' Meg says, as if fleas really might be.

Mr Campbell enters our purchases into the ancient till, one finger, one key at a time. Each price pings up on a card in the yellowed display window. In old money. Shillings and farthings. He does sums on a paper pad, announces our converted bill. He might have made it up. I wouldn't know.

We don't have enough. Mr Campbell's smile straightens into a grimace. We leave without the salmon.

Meg stuffs the shopping inside the trap, gestures for me to pick up my side again.

I don't move.

'Kittens?' I say. 'Why did you lie?' I say. 'I mean, your

Mr Campbell's totally weird, but surely he does leave the shop every now and again. I mean, he knows your grandad. He's lived here forever, right?'

Meg shrugs. 'So?'

'So, he'd know there are otters on the island. And even if he didn't, I don't see him going to the *Daily Mirror* with an announcement.'

Nothing.

'And this war wound . . .'

'That bit's true,' Meg says with a glare that ends the conversation. She grabs the trap and starts to drag it along the ground. 'You helping or not? We can't stand around chatting. We need to find the pups. Make sure they're safe.'

The cute creatures on the shore come sharply into focus: their big round eyes, their carefree play. A stab of worry pushes for space in my too-heavy heart. 'They'll be all right, though, won't they? I mean, surely they're strong enough to survive without their mum?'

Meg shakes her head. 'Otters stay with their mothers until they're around a year old. She teaches them how to hunt for food; how to find fish and eels – all sorts – underwater. How to catch them.' She chews at her bottom lip. 'These pups might only be a few months old. I've seen them catch small stuff: sticklebacks in the river, crawling crabs, things like that, but it's pretty much still play to them.' She lifts her end of the trap, waits for me to lift mine. 'The mum was the main provider, Luke,' she says. 'She's had to spend more and more time away hunting for them as they've grown bigger. This time, she's not coming back.'

A puffin appears in the pale sky, swoops low, floats above us for a moment and sails off into the distance. We both watch it go.

We start to walk even more slowly than before, with the added weight of the shopping. I think of the long, rocky clamber to Puffin Bay, the beach walk to the far side where the hungry babies live. It'll take hours to get there.

'So what now?' I say. 'I mean –' I nod at the bags and tins of fish – 'I mean I want to help and everything, but we can't do a food drop every day, *can* we? And the diving, the hunting and everything. Won't they work that out for themselves – rather than starve?'

Meg stares at me as if I'm missing some glaringly obvious fact. 'They can't. I doubt they're strong enough divers yet. They need to be able to stay underwater for long periods, able to fight it out with some of the "meals" that don't fancy being eaten.' She sighs. 'And they've got to have their wits about them all the time: they're deaf underwater.

Their ears close over down there. Anyway, their coats won't be fully waterproof yet, so they'd get too cold underwater.'

Waterproof coats? An image of small otters in yellow jackets and sou'westers pops into my mind. I push it away. This isn't funny.

And I'm starting to think there's a very serious plan up Meg's sleeve.

I stumble on a large stone. The trap smacks against my shin; brings my first question sharply into focus.

'This trap,' I say. 'It's not just "in case", is it?'

Narrow seabird eyes again. 'Even if starvation doesn't kill those pups, something – someone – else will. Fox. Badger. Wildcat. Eagle.' She pulls ahead, almost jerks my arm out of its socket. 'They won't stand a chance.'

I wince. Meg might be obsessed with animal welfare but she's completely oblivious to mine. I drop my end of the trap. It hits the rocky ground with a metallic shudder. I rub at my arm, wonder how a lumbering seal could ever catch an otter; make a note to ask about the eagle. I'd like to see that. From a safe distance.

'So, assuming they get hungry enough to enter your trap, what then? Where are we taking them? And how, exactly, are you proposing to teach them underwater hunting skills?'

'OK, so the details need working on.' Meg sniffs. 'But this is an emergency action. We can think about all that later. Find a way.'

'We?' I say, not sure I'm ready to be an otter rescuer. What if we get things wrong? *I* don't even know how to rescue my own mother. Or myself.

'Maybe it's better to leave them in the wild,' I say. 'Not to interfere.'

The seabird eyes burn into me, narrower still. Like if I won't help, I'm no better than that winged puffin chick assassin. Or the eagle.

Or my dad.

I grip the cold edge of the trap, heave it off the ground.

I'm in.

Of course I'm in.

*I'm* not the sort of person that walks away.

# NINETEEN

We take the shorter, forest route to Puffin Bay, avoiding the rocky challenge I was dreading. Negotiating the tangle of trees is not easy. Branches snatch at the sides of the trap, twigs hook themselves inside the mesh like bony fingers, scratch at our faces. We go single file through gaps between trees in some places, Meg holding her end of the trap behind her back.

But the place is amazing in the daylight. A riot of colour – every shade of green you could imagine: glimpses of vivid blue sky; yellow spangles of daylight on the mossy floor; rivers of purple heather. A muddle of sound. Bird calls, long and shrill, staccato, soft and sweet. The notes overlap with the tremble of leaves, the snap of wood fragments under our feet. It's a kind of woodland orchestra.

I imagine my fingers on the strings of the old Stratocaster, running up and down its neck, discovering some of the forest notes and rhythms. I see Dad's hands there, feel his own fingers move mine; see his smile of encouragement.

I remember how those strings – the music in them – connected us.

Father and son.

I remember the sharp snap of those strings; the easy splinter of the shiny Stratocaster neck. The easy way Dad walked out on me.

Maybe the connection was never there at all.

I push away the images; push away the pain.

Meg is looking at me. 'You're quiet, city boy,' she says. She lifts an overhanging bough out of her way. I fend it off before it catches me full in the face.

'Those pups,' I say. 'Maybe their dad will find them now.'

'Better hope he doesn't. He's more than likely to finish them off: especially the boy pup. Otter males are territorial. They don't allow rivals in their area.'

'Harsh,' I say. 'Disgusting.'

'It's just nature,' Meg says. 'There are reasons.'

Reasons. I'm sick of 'reasons'.

We press forward, wipe our sleeves across our brows as the day warms.

As we walk, I'm thinking of Dad again. Him and his 'reasons' for leaving, for having his replacement child. I bet in his book that's 'just nature' too.

Resentment sits like a hot stone in my throat. I have the

urge to spit out the burn; to spit out the words, hear them bounce off the ancient trunks and disappear into the air. I glance at Meg.

Might she understand?

She's head down; focused on her mission.

I keep quiet, try to match Meg's determined stride; wrestle with the thought that I'd rather be her than me.

Because even though she's lost both her parents, and that's horrific, neither of them actually *chose* to leave.

The forest thins. Pines give way to beeches and rowan trees. Between them I glimpse the corner of a grey stone building, a rough-cut chimney. Does someone live out here?

'Billy's old croft,' Meg explains. 'Empty now.'

We press on. There's the glint and gurgle of water. The river – or burn, as Meg calls it.

Willow trees bend towards the riverbank or trail their branches into the water like delicate fingers over the edge of a boat. Heather and bracken give way to lush green grass, some of it knee-high. Meg and I have to hoist the laden trap above it. My arms ache more than ever. I can make out the chatter and squawk of puffins in the distance: upbeat, chaotic. An improvised concerto.

Meg points at a fallen tree trunk. She gestures to me to put down the trap, holds her fingers to her lips. 'Their couch,' she whispers. She creeps towards it. I follow.

'No sign,' Meg says. She pushes back the willow curtain, and I see that the surface of the fallen trunk has been partially hollowed out.

'They're here a lot during the day,' Meg goes on. 'The overhanging leaves and branches keep them hidden.' She pushes back grass and leaves with the toe of her trainer, bends, inspects the ground.

'What you looking for?' I ask.

'Sequins,' she says. 'And spraints.'

'What?'

'Sequins: fish scales, bits of eel skin. The odd crab claw. Remnants of an otter kill; if they'd eaten recently, we'd see some around here somewhere. They catch the light. Easy to spot.'

'And spraints?'

'Otter poo: black tarry stuff. Full of bits of eel bones, usually. There's none of that either.' She turns over a flat strip of greying goo with her foot. 'Only old dry bits.'

'Meaning?' I say.

Meg straightens up. Her brow is creased with concern.

'Meaning the pups probably haven't eaten for twenty-four hours. Meaning they haven't been back to their safe place since I was here yesterday.'

Meaning one of those predators might have got to them already.

I look at Meg, see the same thought flicker across her eyes.

'So what now?' I say.

She swallows, hesitates; lifts her chin. 'We go back to the beach,' she says. 'Where we saw them playing. We hope they're there.'

'Right,' I say. 'Right.'

She looks round. 'Help me gather a few branches from over there.' She points at a willow set back from the water. 'We need some camouflage.'

She starts pulling at the lowest-slung branches and twigs.

I stare at her back. '*No way,*' I say. I'm not wearing willow in my hair. Not even for the otters I suddenly *really* want to find.

'Camouflage for the trap, idiot,' Meg says.

I can tell she's grinning, even from behind.

'We'll leave them a meal,' she says, 'in case they come back here while we're away.'

We tuck the trap in close to the willow couch, cover it with leafy foliage. We add a few large stones to prevent the wind from ruining our efforts. We push defrosting eel into the back corner, so that the pups have to go right

153

inside to get at it. Then, Meg explains, the door will snap shut, keeping them inside, and the mean foxes, badgers and eagles out.

In theory.

In reality the stinky fish bait is going to draw a crowd.

One of the 'mean gang' might well get to it first.

If they do, we have to hope they don't hang around.

The tide's well out in the bay. We wait, as we did before, hunched behind the old boat hull, then behind the rocks further out. We wander along the mark of high tide, where the sand is damp, pitted with tiny shells and stones, strewn with weed and other sea debris.

No otters. No fresh 'spraints'.

I look back the way we've come, hoping for the flick of a tail from behind the rocks; a flat nose poking out, testing the air. Hoping *they* might be hiding, watching *us* this time.

I realise how much I want them to be safe; want them to come back with their comical clown antics, their carefree ways that made things seem OK for a few minutes. Hopeful. New.

I don't want that to be broken, too.

Meg glances at me.

'Let's wait a bit longer,' I say.

And we do . . .

There's nothing but the bobbing head of a long-legged beachcomber bird.

'What now?' I say eventually.

Meg doesn't answer. She moves away, squats, peers at something in the sand.

I kneel beside her. Prints. Paw prints. Large ones.

Hopefully, not a wildcat. I glance over my shoulder.

Meg traces one of them with her index finger. 'Otter prints. Five toes.' She sits back on her heels. 'These are the front feet – long claw marks, see? Widely spaced toes. Because of the webbing in between.' She looks up at me, as if the fact that otters have webbed feet is common knowledge.

I nod.

'And these –' she points again – 'these fainter, more smudged ones – hind paws.'

I study them. They all look the same to me. But they're definitely large.

'Not the pups?' I say.

She shakes her head. 'No. An adult. A male, judging

by the size.'

'The pups' dad?' I remember Meg's words about otter fathers, hope this one has more of a sense of responsibility.

Meg nods; sighs. 'Or another male, chancing his luck. Either way, not great, with the pups out here alone.' She scans the bay. 'Suppose they might have wandered further than usual, looking for their mum. Let's carry on a bit, keep our eyes open for any sign. If they are hanging around here somewhere, our best hope is that they hear us coming, make a run for their hideout and find our eel 'breakfast room'.

And if they do, I think, that's great. But *my* best hope is that Meg then has some idea about what happens next. Some *very clear* idea about what we do with two trapped and terrified wild otters that *really* need their mum.

# TWENTY

We find nothing in the bay. And when we get back to the fallen willow, the trap is undisturbed. Meg says it might not mean anything. The otters might instinctively hide out until dusk.

'Makes sense,' I say. But I'm not sure how to feel.

We head home for lunch, agree to check again later.

On the way to the cottage I realise I forgot to leave Mum a note about where I was going. Hopefully, this isn't the time she remembers to worry like she used to. Hopefully, she's actually noticed I'm not there.

She has noticed. But she hasn't been up long enough to worry.

She notices the smell too, the moment I enter the kitchen. I tell her I've been messing about with a dead crab I found, and she smiles and nods; says something old-fashioned about boys being boys. I think of Meg, who blows that kind of idea out of the water all by herself. For a split-second I wonder whether my new sister might be like that too.

We eat a kind of brunch of golden-yolked eggs, beans and fat flat mushrooms. I'm starving, and finish up the last of the bread, thickly spread with jam. Mum promises to go to the shop later to restock. She holds my gaze, as if she's hoping I'll offer to go with her. Or instead of her. I don't. She needs the fresh air, and I need to avoid awkward questions about kittens from weird Mr Campbell. Especially with Mum there. I'm pretty sure she'll freak out at the thought of me tangling with wild animals with huge claws. Even now.

I'm freaking out about that too. Just a bit.

The woods are eerie in the dusk light. We take a slightly different track this time, one that will let us sneak up on the trap unseen, apparently. This way we skirt the standing stone circle Meg promised to show me.

It's spectacular. Five of them, rounded and hunched like ancient hooded figures, grouped around a central taller stone. This one is shaped to a point at the top, like a huge canine tooth. Three round holes are carved halfway up. The low sun shines through each of them, creating long beams of light that stretch towards us. Insects whorl and dance inside them. I stop and stare.

'Amazing, right?' Meg is staring, too. 'Wait till you see the moon rise through those,' she says. 'It's mystical.' She tugs at my sleeve. 'We'll come back, but we have to go. Darkness drops quickly here, as you may have noticed.'

I drag myself away, keep looking over my shoulder. There's something magnetic about these stones. I swear the beams of light are shifting, following us through the trees. It dawns on me that the forest orchestra is silent this time. Strange.

But as we near the riverbank the air is filled with music again. Evening birdsong, the swish and sway of the willow trees, the ripple of the river.

We slow our footsteps as the otter couch comes into sight. Meg looks around, presumably checking for unwanted guests. We creep towards the trap. A twig snaps under my foot, and there's a new sound: thin and reedy. A bit like a mewling kitten.

It comes again, a falling descant of three sad notes.

It's coming from the trap.

Meg lifts a corner of the covering. There's a panicked scuffle as she pulls it back a little further, dislodges a stone weight from the top.

Over her shoulder I see the flat brown head and wiry whiskers of an otter. A small one. River-dark eyes stare back at me, round with fear. The pup presses itself into the back of the trap, as if it hopes to squeeze through the mesh squares. It shakes, shivers. It gives up the escape attempt and curls into a tight, trembling ball. The stench of sun-warmed, soggy eel mixes with something metallic. The smell of fear. Or blood.

'He's terrified,' I whisper. 'Maybe we should just let him go, let him take his chances. Maybe that's kinder.'

'She,' Meg whispers. 'I think. This is the smaller pup. And, no, it wouldn't be.'

She replaces the oilcloth, starts to strip way the camouflage. 'She's hurt. There's blood on her tail and back. Didn't you see?'

I shake my head. 'Badly hurt?'

'I can't see. But she needs help. She looks cold. We need to get her somewhere safe and warm, get her wounds seen to.' She lifts her jacket, pulls a length of thin rope from around her waist. 'Help me tie the oilskin round the trap nice and tightly so she feels hidden away.'

I creep closer, a curl of cold worry in my stomach. I hope we aren't too late. I try not to look at the blood.

We do our best, try to avoid worrying the whimpering

creature inside more than we have to. I manage a couple of knots that meet with Meg's approval.

'Scouts,' I say. 'When I was younger.'

'Keep the trap level as we walk,' Meg instructs. 'Ready?'

I brush bits of bark fragment from my hands. 'Ready,' I say. 'But is the vet's open this late?'

Meg nods to me to lift, ignores my question. 'One of us will have to come back tomorrow,' she says. 'For the second pup.'

Questions tumble around my head as we set off. What if we're making her injuries worse by moving her? What if there's some law against trapping wild otters? What if she dies?

Where, exactly, are we taking her?

But holding the trap steady takes total concentration and all our energy. We keep having to stop and get our breath. The otter baby is silent, the forest filled with snaps and rustles. I worry on both counts.

By the time we reach our side of the island, pain is shooting up and down my arms. I'll never be able to straighten my fingers again. I gesture to Meg that I need a break, rub at raised ridges across my palms. Meg appears fine. As usual. She looks lost in thought.

I nudge her. 'How much further?' I say. 'To the vet's?'

Her face looms closer, a small moon in the semi-darkness. 'We're not taking her to the vet,' she whispers. 'And keep your voice down, remember?' She zips her jacket up to the neck, the sound ridiculously loud in the still of the inky, night-soaked bay. 'Ms Donald – that's the vet – she's on her summer holiday. We'd have to take the ferry to the mainland, and there isn't one until the day after tomorrow.'

'Unbelievable,' I say. This place is unreal.

'There was no vet at all for centuries,' Meg says. 'How d'you think island folk managed then? We've got our own ways, our own remedies.'

I think of Meg's house, the collection of jars and bottles, the specimens I'd rather not know about. 'Suppose,' I say. Mainly because I'm too tired to argue. But the worm of worry inside me loops and twists. I doubt *she's* ever treated a wild otter. And it's not like she can keep it at the boathouse. Not with her grandad . . .

Meg crouches, puts her ear to the trap.

'Should she be this quiet?' I say.

Meg shakes her head. 'Not sure,' she says. There's a tremble in her voice. 'Better get going. And be super-careful on the cliff staircase in this light. One slip and . . .'

'Wait,' I say. 'So where *are* we taking her? Not to yours?'

The seabird eyes glare, cinder-bright in the darkness. 'Grandad can't know we've got her,' she hisses. 'He can't know we've been to Puffin Bay. I thought you got that. And you can *never even mention* otters when he's around. Right?'

I see the old man's eyes again. The terror in them. The tremble in those words: Otters' Moon. The warning in them. 'Not likely to forget, am I?' I say.

'Good,' Meg says.

'So where, then?'

'Yours. The old summerhouse at the end of the garden.'

'No. No way.'

'No choice.' Meg shoves her hands on her hips.

'Not possible,' I say, planting my feet more firmly in the sand. 'I can't look after a sick otter! Anyway, my mum would go ballistic.'

Not necessarily true: I can't be sure she'd notice. She doesn't know there *is* a summerhouse. If she did, she'd tell me to stay out. It's ancient; full of rusted relics.

A weak whimper from the trap intercepts the argument. At the same moment my stomach growls with hunger.

I heave a sigh. 'OK. OK. One night. *One.* But *you're* playing otter night nurse.'

The summerhouse has electric light, which is news to me. A single bulb hangs from the wooden ceiling. It's thick with flies, but it works. Which is just as well. The place is a mess of cobwebs, dust and junk.

'Looks dry, at least,' Meg says.

We leave the trap outside, move aside a rusty mower, a small blue tricycle, faded deckchairs and a tangle of fishing gear. We find some musty blankets in a wicker basket, spread them on the floor. Meg spots a small chipped dog bowl among some plant pots, reaches it down. She magically produces a bottle of water from her backpack. We share half of it. She pours the rest into the bowl.

'Can you refill this from the garden tap?' she says, holding out the bottle. 'So we can wash her wound.'

'It's by the back door,' I say. 'Mum might hear me.'

'Go in. Make an excuse. Watering the plants or something, I don't know. Be better if she knows you're back, anyway, won't it?'

'Suppose,' I say. 'But I'm not as good at lying as you are.'

Meg's cheeks flush. Pink. She looks down. 'Just hurry up,' she says.

I walk across the grass, evening dew already cool through the hole in my trainer. Another reminder of Dad. I'm suddenly sorry for what I said. Meg's 'lies' – her secretive ways – they're all about protecting her grandad; all about keeping him calm and well. More and more, I tell those kinds of lies too. For Mum. About Mum.

And maybe silence is the biggest lie of all.

Mum's conked out on the sofa, so no need for any 'stories' this time. I don't see any wine glasses, so I think she's just having a nap. She naps a lot these days.

She did go to the shop, though. There are fresh rolls on the table, green apples on the dresser. I grab some of both, add a couple of cheese triangles from the fridge; stuff them in a bag. I run to the loo and, while I'm there, rifle through the bathroom cabinet. There's a tiny white box marked 'First Aid' and a roll of bandages. I take those too, add a tube of pink antiseptic that I remember from my skinned-knee days. Hopefully, it's not poisonous to otters.

Meg has dragged the trap inside the summerhouse and is kneeling on a blanket beside it. She's folded back the oilskin so that it covers just one end of the trap. The otter is cowering in the back corner, shaking more than ever.

'Poor thing,' I whisper. 'Still alive, though.' I let out a breath I didn't know I was holding. I hand the water to Meg, spread my other finds on the blanket.

'Thanks.' Meg ignores the food, inspects the contents of the first-aid kit, unrolls the bandage. 'Might be useful,' she says. 'If we can get close enough.'

'Doesn't look like she's got much fight in her,' I say.

'She's a wild animal,' Meg says. 'They're at their fiercest when they're hurt. And scared. She might be a baby, but she'll already have super-sharp teeth. Her front claws will soon be powerful enough to tear apart a rabbit. We'll have to watch ourselves. She doesn't know we only want to help.'

'Otters eat *rabbits*?' I say.

'They eat all sorts. But right now, this one needs fluid more than anything. And we have to check her wounds, clean them if she'll let us.' She produces a pair of battered garden gloves from behind her back. 'Found these,' she says. 'Bit of protection, anyway.'

She unclips the door at the front of the trap. The otter opens her mouth, shows her teeth. Meg's right. Her baby canines are already long and sharp. She makes a frantic chittering sound but stays where she is as Meg slides the water bowl in.

'It's OK, little one,' Meg croons. She withdraws her hand, pushes the door. I hold my breath again, wait. The otter's head sink a little, stretches forward. Her whiskers tremble.

She retreats.

'Maybe if we switch off the light,' I say. 'And go outside for a bit . . .'

'Worth a go,' Meg says.

The garden is filled with inky shadows. A yellow half-moon shows above the cottage roof, but the windows are dark. Mum's still asleep, then.

We sit on a nearby stone bench. Tiny insects zoom in, monotone: buzz around our faces. I bat one from my cheek.

'Wonder what she's doing in there,' I say.

'Not much,' Meg shifts on the cold stone. 'She looks weaker than earlier. She really needs to drink. Especially as she's not eaten, and she's hurt. She'll be wary of the bowl *and* the water; the unfamiliar smells, though, so . . .' Her hands lift and fall, white birds in the moonlight.

A thought strikes me.

'The outside tap,' I say. 'You knew it was there.'

Meg turns away. There's just the insects and the moon and a sudden eerie howl carried on the air.

'Fox.' Meg shifts on the cold stone, bends forward, elbows on knees.

'We lived here,' she says, her voice softer now, a key change. 'Before. All of us: Mum, Dad, Grandad, me.'

'This was *your* house?'

'Still is. Grandad's, anyway. He couldn't stay here after Mum and Dad. He tried. He couldn't. He owned the boathouse too, so he locked this place up and off we went.'

Mystery solved.

'Working on the boathouse, turning it into a home – he says it helped him.'

I think of our house, the only home I've known. The markings on the kitchen door frame that show how I've grown. The apple tree in the garden with low branches for climbing. The pond Dad and I dug together and stocked with glinting golden fish.

'Didn't you miss this place?' I say. 'I mean, with the memories and everything.'

'I was tiny,' she says. 'But, yes. I think so. You saw the drawings in my room?'

I nod. The childish houses with red roofs and wonky windows; the splodges of colour that might be gardens. The stick figures beside them.

'When I was a bit older, I came here sometimes; sat in the garden. Pretended. Then Grandad started renting it out in the summer. We needed the income. So . . .'

I shiver; feel suddenly weird, like Mum and I shouldn't be here. Like we've stolen Meg's life.

Like Jenny stole ours.

How must *Meg* feel?

'You don't mind? I mean, strangers . . .'

She elbows me in the ribs. 'Yeah, city folk. Annoying ones.'

I smile. She smiles, too.

'I come here whenever I want – in between guests. We don't get many. I clean up, do the beds and stuff.' She shrugs. 'The rooms are full of other faces now; other people's lives.' She stands up. 'Other people's memories.'

'Mum. Dad. *They're* in *here.*' She taps her chest. 'Nothing changes that.'

I look away, swallow hard.

Dad's words. When he left. 'I'm still your dad, Luke. Nothing changes that. Even when I'm not here, you and me, we're together in here.' Hand held over his heart. 'Always.'

He didn't make it clear that was the *only* place we'd be together from then on. Or that I'd soon get booted out of there too, by Jenny's shiny new child.

'Luke?' Meg taps me on the arm. 'You OK?'

'Just tired.' I yawn. Convincingly, I think. 'Let's see what happening in the summerhouse.'

We sneak back inside. The otter has moved. Her big eyes glisten halfway down the cage. She freezes when we switch on the light. Crystal drops sit on her whiskers. Water.

I feel the pull of a smile. My idea worked.

'Good girl,' Meg murmurs. 'Is that better?'

The otter turns her head away, tucks it low, like if she can't see us, we can't see *her*. Her thick tail stretches behind her, pokes through the mesh squares at the back of the 'cage'. A gash near the tip oozes bright red.

'Quick,' Meg whispers. 'Pass me the rest of the water.'

The otter remains statue-still as Meg tilts the bottle, lets the water trickle over her wound.

I hand Meg the tube of antiseptic. 'Better not risk it,' she says. 'She'll lick it off. Grandad says boiled water and salt's best. Kills germs and helps healing.'

I glance towards the cottage; can't see it through the thick summer bushes.

Meg shakes her head. 'Morning will do,' she says. 'Bring some then. Hopefully, we've washed most of the dirt out of that wound. That'll have to do for now.' She leans in for a better look.

The otter curls into a ball again, tucks her tail underneath her body.

'Yeah, she's had enough,' I say, remembering my mate

Jed's hamster that died of fright one Fireworks Night. 'Shouldn't we just let her rest?'

Meg nods. 'I need to get back to Grandad.' She pulls a contrite face. 'He thinks I've been for tea with you.'

I raise my eyebrows; hope that's not her way of inviting herself. She delves inside her backpack, produces a tin of plain sardines: the ring-pull kind, fortunately. Although, knowing Meg, she'll have a tin opener in that Mary Poppins bag as well.

'Not ideal food,' she says. 'But it'll have to do.'

We scoop some out with our fingers. Silvery scales and blank eyes stick to our fingers as we poke the slimy fish bodies in through the mesh. I hope they taste better than they look. We cover the trap again, add a blanket for extra warmth and close the door softly behind us as we leave.

Halfway across the lawn, I remember the howl of the fox. I run back and check the summerhouse door.

Just in case.

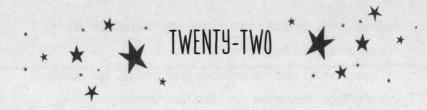
My dreams are invaded by ghosts: a wispy blond-haired mother, a faceless father. A small girl with seabird eyes. They wander around the cottage, drift out through the front door.

The garden becomes a wild ocean. The ghostly family float above the waves, buffeted by a wild wind that blows from all sides. Flying otters emerge in a endless stream from a vast, misshapen moon. I'm snatched from a boat by an eagle with the face of a fox. The moon vanishes, like someone switched out a light.

I'm calling for Dad in the darkness.

He doesn't come.

I jump awake as Meg's mum bends to kiss me on the forehead. The flowery dress from the photograph flutters around her.

Am I sleeping in Meg's old bed?

For a few seconds, my heart beats heavy rock band. I kneel up, push back the curtains. There's an orange and pink dawn, the usual mix of green lawn and overgrown bushes. My breathing slows.

The otter: has she survived the night?

I should probably wait for Meg, but I throw my dressing gown over my pyjamas, shove my bare feet into my trainers. The right one is still damp from last night. *Thanks, Dad.* I kick them off, find Mum's green wellies in the under-stair cupboard instead.

Outside, the grass is scattered with dew diamonds. There's a chill in the air. My feet slide and slap in the too-big wellies. According to Meg, otters have super hearing powers on land, so I slow down, try to make less noise.

I hesitate at the summerhouse door, scared about what I might find. I think of the tiny creature inside, whisked away from everything she knows.

*I* know how that feels.

I grasp the wet doorknob, step inside.

There's no sound from the trap. No scratch or scuffle. Not a whine or whimper.

My hands shake as I roll back a corner of the blanket and oilcloth.

Round dark eyes meet my own. We stare at one another for what feels like an hour: wounded wild otter, displaced city boy. I crouch, rock-still. The air stills too. There's just the quick rise and fall of spiky otter fur; my own double-time breathing. The stench of sardines.

Then, a miniscule twitch of long whiskers.

Another.

The otter stretches her thick neck, just an inch. Wide nostrils flare. She sniffs.

'Hi,' I whisper. I notice last night's tinned supper, dry now; untouched. 'Don't blame you. I don't like the stuff either.'

Her flat head snaps back, but her eyes are steady. She sniffs again, this time in the direction of her empty water bowl.

She's thirsty. Why didn't I think to bring water? Stupid.

'I'm going to have to move,' I whisper. 'Don't be scared, OK?' I get slowly to my feet.

She cowers again, curls into her safety ball. 'Here,' I say, pulling down the covers again. 'Now you're hidden, just like in your willow couch. Won't be a minute.'

I head for the outside tap, hurry back with the morning-cold water. The summerhouse windows burn bright orange in the sunrise. Perhaps summer is finally about to join us here. In August.

Maybe we should find some willow foliage to cover the trap, keep it cool. Maybe to spread like a nest inside. I try to remember if there are willows anywhere near the cottage. Doubtful, on this grey side of the island. Although, to be fair, I haven't been taking too much notice.

Back inside, the otter/boy stand-off is shorter than before. She moves back as I unlatch the door, fill her bowl. This time, there's no panicked hiding of her head. But as she inches forward to drink, her legs tremble. I think of Mum after Dad left. How her legs wouldn't hold her weight when she finally agreed to get out of bed. How she hadn't eaten for three days.

I peer up at the shelves above for food supplies left over from yesterday. A carton of Mr Campbell's kitten milk is tucked next to a battered watering can. I move in slow motion, reach it down.

'How about this?' I whisper. 'Better than sardines?'

I tear off a corner, add the yellowy liquid to her water bowl. The otter stares again; blinks. Her eyelids droop like she's struggling to stay awake.

'Just a sip. Before you sleep.' I move the bowl a little closer to her nose.

A mistake. She's a tight ball again.

I think of our tactic last night; wonder if she'd feel safer – more ready to eat – without me watching this time, too. I slip out into the garden and go in search of my own breakfast. Which will definitely *not* include sardines.

I hope Meg's here when I'm done. With a proper plan.

I don't know anything about otters, but I *do* know we can't keep a wild creature cooped up in here for long. Not if it's going to survive.

I almost miss the knock at the cottage door through the crunch of my cereal. I rush to answer, mouth full of cornflakes. It's still barely eight o'clock. Mum's asleep. What's Meg *doing*?

It's not her.

Mr Campbell stands stiff as a flagpole on the front step, not a hair out of place. *He* looks out of place, though, against the soft shapes of the garden. A penguin in the jungle.

I swallow, wipe milk from my chin.

'Mr Campbell,' I say.

He nods, takes a folded piece of paper from his inside pocket, thrusts it in my direction. 'Urgent message. For your mother. Be sure tae pass it on. Right away, if you please.'

Another nod. He turns on his heel and glides down the garden path.

Man of few words. As ever.

I close the door, lean against it.

Something to do with Dad. Got to be.

I turn the paper over and over, consider scrunching it into a ball and binning it along with the soggy remains of my breakfast.

I unfold it.

Mr James Pensford will telephone at 12.15 today for Mrs Pensford regarding an urgent family matter.

Please attend the shop in good time. Mr Pensford expressly requests that he is able also to speak with his son.

Sincerely,

Alistair Campbell esq.

Proprietor, Campbell's Emporium

*Expressly requests.* Seriously?

No way.

I reconsider the cornflake burial but decide on a different tactic. I set a breakfast place for Mum, refold the note, slip it into the toast rack next to her plate. If she comes down on time, so be it. If not, I'm covered.

Either way, she won't look for me in the summerhouse.

## TWENTY-THREE

I slip outside. Meg's climbing over the garden gate as I close the back door. She's brought more eels and some herrings from the freezer. She was up early, she tells me, to check for any signs of the other otter pup in Puffin Bay. She didn't find any. It's possible he's ventured off to find territory of his own, she says. Apparently, otter mums sometimes abandon young males early, leave them to their own devices. Sometimes they survive that; sometimes not.

'Nature,' she says, 'has its own reasons.'

We agree that whatever nature has to say about it, we're not giving up hope.

The otter has drunk some of the kitten milk.

Her clownish whiskers twitch as Meg unwraps the eel. It's covered in ice crystals.

'You'll have to wait a bit,' I say.

She tips her head to one side, blinks. Tiny squares of sunlit windowpane show in her black button eyes.

Meg smiles. 'She looks a bit brighter. Good call with the milk, city boy.'

I feel a surge of pride. I'm doing something right for once.

I nod. 'Thanks,' I say. 'She can't stay in here much longer, though. It's going to get boiling.' I pull my sweatshirt over my head. 'What's the plan? Where are we taking her?'

Meg chews on a strand of her hair. Today it looks like pale straw, whipped by wind and sea. 'I'm thinking – Billy's croft,' she says. 'It's been closed for years, but Grandad's still got the key.' She screws up her eyes as if trying to focus on something blurred. 'We were always there, Grandad and me, when Billy was around.' She unfolds her legs, careful not to startle the otter, eases a window open. 'She'd be safe. And it's in the woods; close to burn, beach and sea, so she can learn to be a proper otter. With our help.'

'Right,' I say. But I'm wondering exactly how much Meg or I can know about wrestling with river life for lunch, or deep-sea diving skills.

I look at Meg. Her chin is up. I know that Meg.

I try, anyway.

'Shouldn't we, you know, get an adult involved? Get some proper advice? I mean, we've done OK overnight, but –'

'No,' Meg says, the chin even higher. 'There's no one *to*

help.' The chin drops. She fumbles with the hem of her T-shirt. 'Grandad would,' she says, 'if he wasn't so confused now. Because he sees it: sees how all life's part of *us*. How we're responsible for all of it. But folk round here now, they'd make us put her back. Tell us "not to interfere with the wild".' The seabird stare is back. 'Well, I'm not letting the wild win every time,' she says. 'Not without a fight.'

The otter's eyes are on me, too. Deep and dark as caves. Ancient and brand new all at the same time. And I think how Meg's fight for her is also about other lives. Loved lives, lost long ago in Puffin Bay. My heart tightens for them both. Wild otter. Wild girl.

'Right,' I say. 'When are we heading out?' I think suddenly of the note under Mum's plate, feel a stab of uncertainty. 'Only I might have stuff to do for Mum first.'

Right on cue, I hear her call for me. Her voice shifts up and down the scale each time she says my name. I duck my head, without really having decided to do that.

Meg touches my arm, peers at me from under her fringe. I feel the stare of the otter, inches from my face now. I straighten, get to my feet.

'Wait, OK. I'll be back. To go to Billy's.'

Meg shakes her head. 'Not today,' she says. 'Grandad needs me. And anyway, we should keep the pup here a bit longer, let her rest. Carting her around again so soon might be too much.'

I hesitate, hand on the doorknob. But Mum's in the garden, turning this way and that. Her flimsy dressing gown lifts in the air as she moves. She shields her face with one hand, searches; calls again.

The otter calls too. It's a plaintive chirrup, like a baby bird, waiting open-beaked for food. Its helplessness pulls at me. I'm not sure I can leave.

'I'll stay a while,' Meg says. 'Leave her some eel and more water. Now go. Sounds important.'

*No*, I think. *It's not.*

'I'm not talking to him,' I tell Mum. 'I'm keeping you company, that's all.'

Mum smiles her sad 'whatever is right for you' smile; squeezes my hand. She loops her arm through mine as the arched windows of Campbell's Emporium come into view. Maybe to offer moral support to me; maybe to find some for herself. I think of my other life, the one where I wouldn't be seen dead having any kind of physical contact with my mum in public; where I'd have brushed her away, scanned the area for witnesses. I try to recall when I started doing that. And why.

Mr Campbell is standing by the door. He nods his greeting and indicates the phone at one end of the counter. It looks like he stole it from a black-and-white movie set: huge round dial with printed numbers, heavy handset attached by a curly cord. It rings, shrill and sudden at exactly twelve fifteen. Not like Dad to keep his word. Not since *her*.

*Them.*

Mum jumps, reaches to answer. Her hand is shaking.

I grab the receiver and hold it to my ear. I'm not letting him upset her again.

'What?' I say.

My throat closes at the sound of his voice. Heat rises in my face, prickles behind my eyes. I feel like I'm four years old again; like he's ramraiding a portcullis I didn't know I'd built; trying to storm my castle, flaming torch in hand. He's not coming in.

I hand over to Mum; go and stand outside. I kick at pebbles, hate myself for letting her down. Hate Dad more.

I don't know what I wanted him to say. '*Sorry,*' maybe. '*I made a mistake.*'

'*I love you.*'

But, no, just some babble about his shiny new child being sick; how his perfect little bubble just got burst. How he hopes I'll understand why he can't come to visit. He was fighting back tears, I could tell.

They weren't for me.

Like I care. About any of it.

Mum's paler than ever when she comes out. She hands me a Snickers bar, peels the wrapper from one for herself. She stares at it as if she can't remember how it got there.

'Mum?' I say.

She blinks, rearranges her face. 'I'm glad you two talked,' she says.

'*We* didn't,' I say. '*He* did.'

'He's got a lot on his plate, Luke. He's very worried about the baby. But he's worried about you too; sad not to be seeing you.'

I grit my teeth, shove my hands in my pockets; look away.

Her hand lands on my arm again, feather soft. 'Luke?'

I swing round. 'Don't you dare, Mum. Don't even try to make excuses for him. Why do you always do that? He only thinks about himself.'

Mum sighs. We walk in silence. I nibble at the chocolate, shoot quick glances at Mum. She looks all right for once. Maybe she's covering up. Or maybe, just maybe, she's starting to get over him . . .

She stares up at the newly bright sky. 'I might take my camera out again,' she says. 'Explore a bit more of the island in this light.'

'You should,' I say. 'Good idea.'

Could just be a Mum tactic, I think. To get me to talk. I won't.

'Come with me?'

I bite my lip; wonder what to do. I don't want to discourage Mum from getting out. But I can't let the otter down either. Or Meg.

'Not sure. Maybe,' I say, playing for time.

A cluster of gigantic crows make up my mind for me. They land in front of us on the cottage fence, line up like black notes on sheet music. They bend their heads together as we approach: gossiping, no doubt. Or agreeing a plan. All but one of them take off before we get close, a rabble of wingbeats and raucous caws. They regroup in the nearest tree. The remaining bird hops on to the grass, begins a slow walk in the direction of the summerhouse. He's followed by several pairs of yellow-bead eyes.

Meg will be gone by now.

I'm not leaving that baby otter on her own.

## TWENTY-FOUR

Meg has left the summerhouse window cracked open for air. I'm pretty sure that's all it took to summon the band of brothers outside. It will have to stay shut when neither of us is here. For now, if I'm to breathe through the eel/otter fumes, it needs to stay open.

Meg's found a child's blackboard from somewhere (hers, presumably) and left me a message.

Back soon as I can. Give pup more milk/water every couple of hours. More eel in flowerpot. Watch out for her teeth, city boy.

I settle down on a blanket. The otter studies me. I study her. I take in her hooded eyelids, her small low-set ears, her wide nostrils. She chitters at me. I wonder what that means; wonder whether she's afraid she's stuck in that trap forever – never to glide in the cool of the burn again; never to rest in her wild willow home.

185

Whether she wonders why her mum has left her alone.

I wish I could speak otter; tell her she's not all alone. Tell her things will be OK again.

'I'm sorry,' I say, 'Willow.' Because, clearly, that has to be her name.

After a while, she falls asleep with her chin in her water bowl. I escape to the clean air, lie on the grass outside the door. The crows have gone. For now. There's the lazy hum of bees and, somewhere close by, a tuneful songbird. I watch a tiny insect scale a blade of grass and push away the sound of Dad's voice; push away the news that my tiny 'sister' has 'an uphill battle' of her own, the thought that she's as innocent as the wounded orphan curled safely in her cage. The thought that she might need me, too.

I feel like someone's sitting on my chest, pressing my ribs against my lungs so it's hard to breathe. I count slow breaths in and out, focus on the drift of the sky, and somehow I fall asleep too.

Meg wakes me with a prod of her trainer and her bubble of a laugh. We check on the otter and agree to move her to Billy's in the morning. We even agree on her name. Although Meg does give me a raised-eyebrow smile. Maybe naming wild creatures is too Disney for a serious marine biologist.

I walk with her to the cliff steps.

She skips down the first few, stops; calls up. 'You OK, city boy?'

I give her a thumbs up and wander back for some supper. As I wash my hands, I wonder how Meg knew that just now I'm *anything but* OK.

I check my face in the mirror and head for the kitchen, determined not to let Mum see through me like Meg did. If she's still feeling brighter, I don't want to spoil things.

I chop celery, carrots and onion for bolognese. Mum sautés minced beef and adds glistening tomatoes from a tin. Over the sizzle of the pans, she talks about the baby again. About her heart. She wants to be sure I've understood the situation.

'I get it, Mum, OK?' I stir the vegetables a bit faster. 'She has holes in her heart. She needs operations to fix them and she can't have them till she's bigger, stronger. She might not survive until then.' I turn up the heat under my pan. 'I just don't see what it's got to do with me.' The vegetable sizzle grows louder, fat hisses and spits over the flame.

Mum says something that I can't hear. Her cheeks are flushed, her eyes full of concern when she looks at me. In that moment I wish I could close off my ears like an underwater otter. I don't want to talk about this baby interloper, and I don't want to care about her either.

She isn't the only one with a broken heart.

She's one of the bullets that blew holes in mine.

Mum's taken one of her tablets, so she'll sleep soundly until morning. Maybe right *through* the morning. I can't drop off at all. Sick of tangled sheets and tangled thoughts, I go down for a glass of milk.

I stand at the kitchen window to drink. Moonlight casts long tree shadows on the grass. The cottage presses in on me. I'm suddenly desperate to escape.

I open the back door. Night air lifts the small hairs on my arms. A white moth brushes my face, floats into the hall.

I listen, but the garden is silent. I wonder whether Willow is awake too. Whether night sounds that only she can hear are making her afraid. I nip back to my room, pull on a sweatshirt and socks, grab my sleeping bag from under the bed. It smells faintly of earth and forest floors. More memories of Dad. I look in the wardrobe in case the cottage has others for guests. It doesn't. I'm stuck with my own. Stuck with *him*.

There's panicked scuffling as I enter the summerhouse. I don't put on the light.

'Only me,' I say, and roll back the covering of the trap just far enough for her to see me.

All I can make out is the huge eyes, luminous in a beam of moonlight, and the pale fur under her neck. I get into my sleeping bag, curl up next to her, hoping that my presence is a good thing now, not a source of more fear. She edges closer to the mesh that separates us, gives me a long stare, then curls into a ball.

'I won't hurt you,' I whisper. 'I'll just stay here. Till it's light.'

My body grows heavy, but each time I feel myself slipping into sleep Willow's minor-chord, three-note call pulls me back. I don't have to speak otter to know that she misses her family; misses the safe warmth of home.

Me too.

I unlatch the door of her cage. She uncurls. Her eyes meet mine. She inches forward.

I think of those teeth that one day will bite through the bones of a rabbit. Imagine Meg's derisory 'stupid city boy' stare when Willow crunches through a couple of my toes. I push the door to again.

Willow slumps. Her whimper flattens, like she knows

189

it's hopeless, knows she's totally alone now. An image of another baby slips into my head: dark-haired like me; all alone in the flash and bleep of a hospital night. I pull the cage door wide.

I shuffle down into my sleeping bag, lift it right up to my nose. I wait, eyes fixed on the gaping silver mouth of the trap.

After what seems like hours, Willow's snout appears.

And disappears.

She does this on repeat, then: nothing. Perhaps she's decided better of it. Perhaps she's fallen asleep. I ease myself up on my elbows to take a closer look. As I do, her dark shape shoots out of the trap and vanishes among the stacked clutter at the back of the building.

Brilliant. Now what?

I push my feet into my trainers, worry that no trainer in the world would be a match for otter teeth, let alone Dad's cheapskate versions. I flick on the overhead light.

More panicked scuffling. A stack of plastic chairs teeters, a plant pot topples over, rolls towards me. I'm making things worse by the minute.

Willow's basically nocturnal, I remember. She can do this all night. But she'll be happier in the darkness, at least. I switch off the light.

I'm *not* happier in the darkness.

I try coaxing: a collection of sounds as otter friendly as I can manage. I try staying quiet and still. I feel for another carton of kitten milk – dislodging a second plant pot as I do; need the light on again while I clear the sharp fragments from the floor.

My head thumps. Meg will be here in a few hours. She's going to kill me.

But then again, it's me chancing my big toes in the middle of the night, not her. Even though this whole otter rescue was *her* idea. Maybe I'll just go back to bed, let island girl sort this one with her superior Dr Dolittle knowledge.

Visions of Willow squished under a pile of deckchairs or tangled in the mower blades flit through my mind. I can't leave her.

I pour milk into her bowl, leave it just inside the door of her cage. I shuffle back down into my sleeping bag, wrap it mummy-tight around me. Only the very top of my head is exposed: I want to keep my nose.

I doze; jump awake: another repeat cycle.

I'm in doze mode when it happens: the scratch of claws on the wooden floor.

The tentative feet on my left thigh. I stop breathing. My heart jumps into my ears, a booming 'presto' beat. Surely Willow hears it too. Her warm weight moves to the middle of my chest. Settles.

Minutes go by. I fight the urge to wriggle further out of reach and surface a fraction, so that my eyes are clear of the top of the sleeping bag – nose still under wraps. I don't want to be taken by surprise.

Willow's own nose is inches from my face. Her blackcurrant eyes gleam. Her long whiskers glint silver in the half-light. We blink. Then we are still, suspended somewhere secret; unknown. I sense her fear. She senses mine. It's a sort of meeting place.

She creeps forward. Her whiskers tickle my forehead. I breathe in her fishy breath, feel the flicker of her tiny heart against my throat. Then she moves away, turns around a few times, settles across my thighs. I feel her breathing slow through the thin fabric covering me.

She's sleeping.

She trusts me.

A tear makes it way down my cheek. I lie still, let it run over my chin and down inside the neck of my sleeping bag. There's no one to see.

Somehow, I sleep too. I wake to brilliant strobes of

daylight and one numb ear pressed against the hard summerhouse floor. I'm on my side. And Willow is nestled snuggly in the hollow behind my knees.

# TWENTY-FIVE

We're halfway to Billy's croft and Meg still hasn't shut up about my 'reckless behaviour with a wild otter'.

'I reckon you're secretly impressed,' I say. 'Especially that I still have all my body parts.' I hold up my fingers. 'Look. Want to count my toes as well?'

The seabird eyes are more 'eagle' today. 'She might have injured herself. She might have chewed her way out through the wall while you were having your cosy nap.'

'She didn't,' I say.

'We might never have caught her again.'

'We didn't have to,' I say.

Willow had taken herself into her cage as soon as she smelled the fresh herring Meg brought for her breakfast. Stomach full, she'd gone straight back to sleep. She'd barely moved since, even during the jostling, jiggling journey so far.

'She needed reassurance,' I say. 'She's positively zen now.'

'Zen?' Meg screws up her nose. A small smile twitches at the corners of her mouth.

I shrug. 'Why not?'

She shakes her head. 'City boy turns otter charmer,' she says. 'Who knew?'

I smile. Not me, that's for sure.

'Seriously, though,' Meg says. 'Otters don't behave like that. They're among the wildest of creatures. They keep themselves to themselves.'

'I have charisma,' I say.

Another twitch of a smile. A raised eyebrow.

'Maybe Willow just hasn't learned to fear humans yet,' I add.

Meg nods. 'Maybe. But she needs to. If she's going to survive back in the wild.'

Billy's croft is a low once-white stone building with a drooping wooden lean-to at one side.

That, according to Meg, is – was – the loo. The door is missing now, and the forest has sent long root runners and creeping plants to reclaim the rest of the wooden structure.

'Doesn't matter,' Meg says. 'Out here.'

She's right. The place has a fairy-tale feel. Like no one's been this way for years.

Pale pink roses cover the entire front wall of the croft. Ivy-clad tree stumps sit in a mossy clearing in front. The burn sparkles along one side; widens into a clear pool that looks inviting even to a city boy like me. It's surrounded by clumps of dense silvery weed. Bright yellow and blue flowers sit among them on long flagpole stems.

'Flag iris,' Meg says.

I nod. 'Perfect,' I say.

We peel back creepers from the door to the house. Meg produces a huge black key. It turns with a rusty clunk. The door sticks, scrapes on the rough stone floor as we shoulder it open. We carry Willow's cage inside and set it down.

There's a smell of must and damp and emptiness. Spiders have gone to town. Thick grey webs hang from the ceiling like sad Christmas decorations, looped between sparse bits of furniture: a table, a broken rocking chair, a rusted metal bed frame. An enormous chimney stack spreads across one wall. A fireplace gapes in the middle. A collection of pots and pans cluster around it, all encased in spider netting. A blackened kettle hangs from a giant hook.

'All we're missing is the witch,' I say.

But it's OK, I guess. More space than the summerhouse. More private.

Meg hasn't heard. She seizes on an old tin bath propped against the wall. 'Yes!' she says with a baffling note of excitement in her voice. 'Brilliant.' She nods, drags it down. 'I hoped this was still here. Just what we need. We can fill it from the burn. Just need a bucket or two.' She looks around. 'Or we can use these pots.'

She stands up, hands on hips. 'First, though, we need Billy's lamb fences. You check on Willow, give her a drink.' She shoves her backpack into my arms. 'I'll check out back.'

'Wait,' I say. 'Tin bath. Lamb fences. Explain.'

Meg stares at me. 'Willow can't stay in that trap,' she says, like I'm from another planet. 'And she can't run loose in here. Too many escape holes. And hazards.'

I sigh. 'The lamb thingies.'

She nods. 'Billy kept a few sheep. Most people did, back in the day. If there were orphaned lambs, he brought them in here, kept them warm. I used to come over and feed them from a bottle.' She smiles. 'Funny little things. Grandad and Billy made an indoor pen for them: wood panels with chicken wire. They must be here somewhere. Maybe out back.'

'And the bath?'

'Otters can't be otters without water, city boy. They need to swim. Willow needs to develop her muscles; practise her skills as much as possible. She's got her own pool outside,' she says. 'And the burn and sea just over the dunes. It's perfect. For when she's ready.'

I cross to the window, rub at the filthy pane and peer outside, wonder when *I'll* be ready to let her roam free out there.

'The bath is for now,' Meg says. 'Until she's stronger and more used to us being around. We can't risk her bolting yet.'

'*No*,' I say, 'we can't.'

We find Billy's lamb pen folded up in a ramshackle shed at the back of the croft. The wood is mildewed, the mesh red with rust. We clean it down with old rags soaked in the pool, stand it outside in the sun to dry while we feed herrings to Willow. We find one bucket, choose the largest pan from the witch's fireplace and slog back between pool and tin bath. Willow watches us, head on one side. Her whiskers twitch and quiver. She makes sounds: squeaks and whistles. I worry about the memories carried in the air here, with her seaside playground so close by. Whether she thinks her mother is close by too. Thinks she's coming for her.

Bath full almost to the brim, we position the lamb pen around it. We lift up one side panel and push Willow's cage inside, as far away from the bath as possible. I lean in and unlatch the door.

Meg produces a flask of soup from her bottomless backpack. 'To share,' she says.

I remember the hasty sandwiches I shoved in mine earlier.

'These too if you want,' I say. 'Bit squashed. And the bread might be stale.'

Meg unwinds her headscarf, spreads it on the dusty floor like a mini spotted tablecloth. 'My favourite sort,' Meg says. 'Put them here.'

The sandwiches – and my jeans – are drowned in a deluge of pond water as Willow launches herself into the bath. Her nose rises over the rim for a moment, as if to make sure we're watching. We stand up. She dips down. She twists, turns, tumbles, undeterred by the limitations of a five-foot bath. The water slides back and forth, rears over the sides in giant waves, sploshes on to the floor. Meg and I stand there, puddles around our feet, oblivious to our dripping clothes and soggy feet. Willow is dazzling. I can't wait to see her in the pool.

Meg was right. Otters need to swim.

Her head pops up again. The tub tsunami settles. She plops over the side, shakes out her coat like a dog. Her wet fur stands in spikes all over her body, as if she's gelled it.

'Punk otter,' I say.

Meg laughs.

Willow rolls on to her side, wriggles on her back like a foal in a field. Or my mate Jez's dog, delighting in discovered fox poo.

'She's trying to dry herself off,' Meg says. 'She'll have half the contents of the bath in that thick topcoat. It's water repellent – adult coats are, anyway.' She magically produces a towel from her bag, throws it down in the pen. Willow sniffs at it, scratches it into a heap, rolls among the folds.

'Clever girl,' Meg says.

'Maybe we should get her outside in the sun,' I say. 'She can't dry off properly in here. What if she catches a chill or something?'

'Quite right, Nurse Luke,' Meg says. 'We need her back in the cage.'

'Food should do it,' I say, ignoring the jibe. 'If she's anything like me after a swim. Let's put some herring in there.'

Willow cooperates. She pounces on the herring, pins it down with her front paws and tucks in. Meg and I carry her cage outside, rest alongside it in a patch of sunlight near the edge of the pool. Sunlight skips and dances on the surface. A huge dragonfly hovers nearby on electric-blue wings. A quick, dark shape glides beneath him. A vivid green frog leaps from the reeds, plops into the water. Willow snaps to attention at the sound, a herring fin dangling from her whiskers.

'You any good at fishing?' Meg says. 'We need to do some soon. Grandad thinks I'm doing midnight raids on the fridge: having a "growth spurt". And Mr Campbell is asking questions about the size of the kittens we're feeding.'

'OK, I guess.' I shrug. 'If you count catching the odd tadpole and some sticklebacks.' I remember blunt black bodies bumping against the sides of a jam jar; the twist and jump of silvery fish in the bottom of a net. I remember Dad promising to take me river fishing this summer. Just the two of us. Before baby D-Day. Another of his empty promises. I stand up, stare into the water.

'Any eels in here?' I say.

Meg shakes her head. 'Not in the summer. They swim in during spring, lay their eggs in the burn. They've all headed back out to sea now.' She joins me at the water's edge. 'That's why I've had to bring frozen. Willow might manage to catch frogs and some small fry in here,' she says, pointing to the pond, 'but we'll need to take the boat out, do some sea fishing if we're going feed her properly.'

'Boat?' I say. 'What boat?'

'Billy's,' she says. 'I'll show you. Let's get Willow tucked up inside. She looks dry now.'

'You mean take a boat out *here*, in Puffin Bay?' I say. The loss of her family, the tales of capricious weather press inside my head. 'Is it safe? I mean, can you even sail?'

She stands, hands on hips. 'It's not sailing.' She sighs. 'Billy's is a fishing boat. And we'll be fine. As long as we go in daylight. I've been out loads of times. To the lighthouse, mainly. Now, you helping with Willow, or what?'

I sigh, too. I suppose Meg knows what she's doing. And we will need fresh fish for Willow. Plenty of it.

We give Willow the last of the herrings. She watches us collect up our things.

'You sure she's OK here on her own?' I say. 'Overnight, and everything?'

'She's a lot safer here than she'd be outside.' Meg stuffs the wet towel in her bag, picks up her unopened flask of soup. 'Want some of this before we go?'

I shake my head.

When we open the door to leave, Willow rushes to the end of the pen. She chitters, runs back and forth.

She rears up on her hind legs, showing her pale underbelly. She calls.

'Just a minute, Meg,' I say. I untie my sweatshirt from around my waist – my new one, a birthday present from Mum. I push it inside the cage. 'I'll be back, Willow,' I whisper. 'Very soon.'

Her three-note lament follows us halfway to the dunes. She thinks we've abandoned her. My feet drag heavily in the sand.

Meg puts her hand on my arm. 'No good going back only to leave again,' she says. 'We'd just make things worse.'

She's right. I shove my hands in my pockets and follow Meg over the rise of the dunes.

Billy's boat sits between two of them, anchored to a bleached tree, and covered in tarpaulin. It's a simple fishing boat, two bench seats, two sea-weathered oars resting in metal 'cups' on each side. There's a resident clutch of limpets, but otherwise it looks to be in much better shape than his house. Which is a relief.

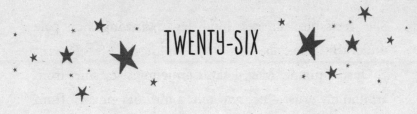

# TWENTY-SIX

We take the boat out the next morning, while Willow takes a post-herring nap. Meg has come equipped with her grandad's fishing rods, a box of rainbow-feathered bait hooks and a wide-mouthed bucket. We wedge them in the space between the two seats, manoeuvre our feet in beside them. It's a squeeze. I scrutinise the interior for cracks or holes that Meg has missed; worry about ending up in a watery grave along with Seth's ghostly sailing crews and the bones of unlucky smugglers.

The sea is calm, the breeze soft. Meg handles the boat like it's an extension of herself. To my surprise I get the hang of rowing in no time. The rhythmic action, the gentle lift of the waves beneath us soothes my nerves. I start to relax.

'You're a natural, city boy.' Meg's eyebrows shoot up in an arc. She grins. 'Who knew? Let's see what kind of fisherman you make.' She drops anchor, shows me how to lock the oars in their rests. 'We're a bit stuck if we lose those,' she says.

I watch her fix a yellow-and-pink bait hook; follow the arc of the line as she casts it high in the air. She's learned from a master. I fumble with my own hook, stab the end of my thumb, draw a red bead of blood. I struggle to balance when I stand to cast my line, almost throw myself into the sea too. But I do it. I feel a smile spread across my face.

'Not such a city boy after all,' Meg says.

We float there, wait for the tug of hungry fish. Gulls circle, snow-white against seamless blue. Wide ocean, wide sky. I think suddenly of the baby, who might never see either of them. I look at Meg, who is so much a part of both.

I realise that somehow we're friends now: city boy and irritating, wild island girl.

'What?' she says, looking at me from under her fringe, like on that first day.

'Nothing,' I say.

But suddenly I want to tell her. About the baby. About Dad.

And I do.

She listens, nods.

'What's her name?' she asks. 'Your sister?'

I shake my head, shrug. 'How should I know?'

Meg trails her fingers in the water. The sea rises over her wrist, pulls back again. 'You *should* know,' she says.

'And you *have* to go and see her. Soon.'

'Why would I want to do that?' I say, a tiny bite of guilt in my stomach. Even if I *did* want to, I couldn't. Couldn't do that to Mum.

'You have to see that baby because right now, you still *can*,' she says. She shakes her hand dry. She turns to face me, the entire ocean in her eyes. 'Don't waste it, Luke. Don't waste time . . .'

My fishing line jerks in my hand. We both jump; gasp.

'Reel it in,' Meg shouts. 'Lift the rod higher.'

A silver-grey fish flips and flops on the water, writhes in the air on the end of my line; lands in the bottom of the boat. I watch it gasp for breath and fight the urge to throw it back, like the sticklebacks and tadpoles.

'Coley,' Meg says. She snatches it up, removes the hook from its gaping mouth. I turn away, remind myself this is for Willow, not for sport. When I look back, the fish stares up at me from the bottom of bucket, glassy-eyed. Still.

'You have to be quick,' Meg says. 'So they don't suffer.'

Her own line twitches and pulls. Mine does the same. The fish keep coming. I wonder why they don't watch and learn, speed away in the other direction. I'm glad they don't, for Willow's sake, at least. We head for shore with four of the silver coley, three tiger-striped mackerel

and a couple of small pearl-grey fish that Meg thinks
might be sprats. Enough food to keep Willow going for
a couple of days.

'I wish my dad could see all this,' I say.

'Tell him,' Meg says. 'What's to lose?'

*Hope*, I think. *That's what.*

The hope that I might still be able to make my dad proud.

The hope that he might actually still care.

Willow considers our first mackerel offering for a moment,
pushes at it with her nose. Then she clutches it between her
front paws, peels back the skin with her sharp teeth, and
tucks in. I draw the line at dangling fish guts and look away.

The whole thing is gone in minutes. Willow sniffs
around, makes sure she hasn't missed any juicy morsels,
cleans her whiskers and feet like a satisfied cat. Only she's
not satisfied. She's soon climbing up the side of her pen.
Her peeps and whistles grow louder, sharper in pitch, and
they're directed at me, judging by her fixed, hypnotic stare.

She's still shouting after a grey 'sprat' dessert.

'She wants out,' I say. 'Shall we try?'

We release her. She scurries under the table, surveys

the scene from there for a while, nose and whiskers twitching. She shoots across the floor, begins another survey from between my feet. Her mackerel breath hits my nostrils. She gives my left trainer a quick nip, then she's everywhere. On Billy's bed, under Billy's bed. In the hearth, where she sends pots and pans clattering across floor; frightens herself back under my chair. She disappears halfway into Meg's bag, all the way into mine. She emerges with a Snickers wrapper in her mouth. She heads for the fish bucket. I grab it just in time. Her finale is a running dive at the tin bath, where she treats us to another swimming masterclass. This time we stand back, stay dry.

Well, Meg stays dry. Willow jumps out, does her wet dog shake at my feet, then lies across them. At least half the contents of the bath seeps into my shoes. I ease them free one at a time, ring out the laces.

'My socks are soaked through!' I say. 'Thanks, Willow.'

Meg laughs. 'Quite an honour,' she says. 'Otter boy!'

I grin. These soggy socks are special. Willow and I, we're family.

I remove one of them, throw it in Meg's direction. It lands just short, with a splat. I think of the water-bomb wars that got Jez and me sent out of science class. I wonder what he's up to back at home; what he'd think of my summer companions: wild otter, wild girl.

Maybe he'd be jealous. Not that he'd ever admit it.

I pad about, making wet footprints on the dusty floor. I set Willow's carnage to rights.

Willow follows me, adds webbed smudges to my own foot floor art. She completes it with another of her full-body rolls.

'She's still sopping,' Meg says. 'Better take her back out in the sun.' She nods at my wet prints. 'You too, merboy.'

'Very funny,' I say.

Willow peers up at me from between my feet, as if poised for our next move.

Meg smiles. 'Looks like she's glued there.' She walks to the door, pulls it open. 'Time to meet the big outdoors again, Willow,' she says.

Willow stares through the gap, whiskers vibrating. I feel her body tense between my ankles. My own body tenses too. What's Meg doing?

'Close it, Meg! She'll get out!'

Meg shakes her head. 'I reckon she'll stay close to her new "mum". Let's try. She belongs out there.' She throws the door wide and walks through it. 'Otter school starts here,' she calls. 'Come on, little one.'

Willow dashes outside, stops, waits. She stands with a front paw raised. Her head whips from side to side, checking for lurking danger.

'It's OK,' I say. I amble over to join Meg at the edge of the pool, try to look confident. Willow needs no further encouragement. She slides into the water and dips down, leaves widening rings on the satin surface; disappears.

I shade my eyes with my hand. No sign of Willow in the now still water.

'*Told* you this was a bad idea,' I say. My heart thunders in my chest. Where *is* she?

Have we lost her for good?

Meg points to a large clump of reeds a few yards out. 'There,' she says. 'Look.'

A triangle of silver bubbles drifts towards us.

'Pockets of air released from her coat,' Meg says.

Seconds later, Willow's flat head appears. 'Phew,' I say. I blink to clear my watery eyes, watch her easy glide to the bank. My drumbeat pulse slows. Meg and I grin at one another like proud parents. As if to up her game, Willow flips over on to her back, rests her short front legs on her belly, and floats there, with smooth sideways flicks of her tail. She looks like a cartoon creation. Otters, they're *amazing*. What else can they do? If there was a half-decent internet connection, I could research them, find out more.

Never mind. Willow and I, we can discover things together. It'll be fun.

After a while, Willow clambers up the bank and treats us to a shower of pond water. She completes her wriggle-rub drying regime, settles on a tree stump to snooze. We rest there, all three of us, in warm sunshine. A birdsong trio plays, rises above the sing of the sea beyond the dunes. I turn my head, study Willow. She opens one eye, chitters softly, closes it again. I smile. My own eyelids droop.

I'm woken by a sharp dig in my ribs. I sit up, rub at my face. It feels sore. I'll get the sunscreen lecture from Mum. If she notices.

'Hurry up,' Meg says, hastily pulling on her trainers. 'We're late.'

'What for?'

'Just late. What time do you think it is?' She pulls off her headband, pushes strands of damp hair from her forehead.

I blink. Get my bearings. The air has cooled now. Clouds of insects hover over the pond, like steam. The sun is sliding towards the dunes.

'Late,' I say. 'You're right.'

Meg swipes at me with her hairband, twists it back around her head.

Willow trots meekly back into the croft with the lure of a striped mackerel in front of her nose. We settle her in her pen with fresh water and dry bedding, grab our bags and run.

We're both quiet on the way home, worries about other responsibilities growing with our distance from the croft. The easy warmth of our day slips away with the sun. Twigs snap and pebbles skitter under our quick, anxious feet.

Have either of us stayed out too long?

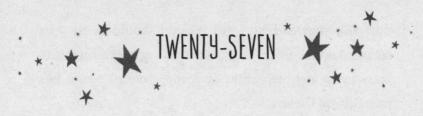

# TWENTY-SEVEN

I hop over the back gate, hurry over the lawn, kick off my trainers inside the door. The hall clock strikes nine. I'm in for more than the sunscreen lecture. I hope I am.

Mum's standing in the kitchen, clutching a cup to her chest door. Her face is white; tear-stained. She slumps down at the table, tries to stifle her sobs with her hand. I see that the white band where her wedding ring used to be is faded, almost gone now.

'I'm really sorry, Mum,' I say. I sit beside her, cover her other hand with mine. 'Sorry I worried you.'

I pat my pockets for a clean tissue, feel only a flat fold of paper: the note I meant to leave her this morning. Great. I hold it out. 'Too late for this?' I say.

Mum unfolds it, reads. She pulls a soggy tissue ball from her sleeve, picks at it.

'Mum?'

She takes a ragged breath, lifts her eyes to mine. '*I'm sorry,*' she says. She shakes her head. Her lips tremble. 'All this with your dad, and just when I should be in your corner, I'm like this. Too busy worrying about myself to know what my own child is doing. To make sure he's safe. Selfish. Useless.'

'What? Mum, no! Dad's the selfish one. You're . . . you're just . . . sad. And that's down to him too.'

She shakes her head 'It's not –' She bites her lip. 'It's not that simple, Luke. I think you know that, really.'

'No,' I say. 'I don't.' No way is Mum taking the blame. Her being sad – ill – that's a reason for Dad to stay, not his excuse for leaving. I pull my chair closer, put my arm around her shoulders. 'And I'm fine, Mum. I'm old enough to look after myself.'

Mum finds one of her watery smiles, touches a finger to my red cheek. 'You still forgot the sunscreen,' she says.

'Point taken,' I say.

I smile back. She noticed.

But Mum's face is serious again.

'That shopkeeper came by again,' she says. 'Mr Campbell.'

'Another call from Dad?'

Mum shakes her head. 'A telegram. An update on the baby. She's having a preliminary op tomorrow. Nothing too much to worry about, but, well, she's so tiny.'

I look down at my knees, trace damp pond-water stains

with my finger. I think of Willow, stronger by the day. My small shadow.

'She'll be all right, won't she?' I say.

Mum nods. 'She should be, I think. I guess your dad just wanted to keep you up to date.'

'Right,' I say, wondering why he bothered. Seeing as I told him I don't care.

'Mr Campbell mentioned a girl. Meghan, is it?'

I shrug. 'Meg. So?'

'So you don't need to keep things from me, Luke,' she says, waving my dishonest note in the air. 'It's OK for you to have fun. I'm happy if you're making friends; finding adventures. Especially now.'

I wince. *Finding adventures.* She thinks I'm five years old. Ironic. Most of the time she's the child and I'm the parent.

'I don't need to tell you everything,' I say. 'I'm not a little kid any more.'

'No,' Mum says. Her mouth sinks at the corners. She dabs at her eyes. 'You're an amazing young man. Go on enjoying some freedom while we're here.' She waves my note in the air. 'But I do need to know where you are. Go beachcombing, fish from the rocks. But, *please*, be careful. Mr Campbell's lived here all his life. He told me things. There've been accidents . . . tragedies.'

I shake my head. 'Stories, Mum. This place is steeped in them.' I laugh. It doesn't sound right. 'Most of them aren't true,' I say, trying for a reassurance I don't feel.

Mum's grip tightens. Her thin fingers dig into my own.

'Promise me two things, sweetheart, OK? You stay out of fishing boats. And *whatever* happens, you keep to *this* side of the island. Understood?'

'Yes,' I say. Because strictly speaking, that's not a lie.

I wrap my hands around hers; remember when mine were small and hers were large and there was only one kind of truth. The memory stings. But I smile into her eyes because she remembered. About the sunscreen. About rules. About being Mum.

I persuade her to go for a bath while I cook pizzas for dinner. When I hear the water running, I nip into her room. Dad's telegram is tucked under a china bowl on the dressing table.

My sister's name is Iris.

I crawl under my bed, blow dust and a surprised red spider from my laptop. Miraculously, there's internet.

Three emails from Dad. My fingers hover over the

mouse pad. I click on the second message – the one with attachments.

And there she is.

Iris.

Indigo eyes. Black tufted hair. Furious fists. Skin so fine her blue veins show through like rivers on a map.

I click again. Dad holds her close. Their faces touch, hers a softer, unfinished version of his.

Of mine.

There's a photo just like it on the dresser at home. What *was* home.

Dad. And newborn me.

I think of tomorrow's surgery, of Iris's tiny broken heart. I wonder whether Dad's will break too when the swing of the theatre door steals her away.

Why it stayed in one piece when he closed the door on me.

My throat tightens.

I flip back to the first image. I leave it open. When I try to sleep, the indigo eyes watch me from the bedside cupboard; become Meg's seabird-blue; Willow's river-deep stare. I see finger trails in the ocean; silver-splashed rings widening on a pond, the tremble of the flag iris, the lift of the blue-winged dragonfly. The soar of gulls over sand formed from millions of shelled lives. Seth is right. Everything is part of everything else.

Me and Iris, we're part of one another. Whether we like it or not.

I'm up early, keen to get back to Willow. To push away worries about Iris and her hovering heart. They hurt.

Mum's up and about too. Her camera equipment is spread on the lounge table. She's taking a lead from me, she says, getting out to do some exploring of her own, hoping for some good shots. Perhaps *she's* worrying about Iris too. Her own heart is cracked open, but it still bleeds for everyone else. No matter what she tells herself.

'Want me to come with you?' I say, terrified that she does. Willow needs me.

She waves her hand. 'I'm fine, love,' she says. 'Go and have fun.' She points at the window, already lit by yellow rays. 'Just remember the sunscreen this time.' She tightens the cap on a long lens, looks up at me. 'And what we agreed.'

I nod, look quickly away. 'What do you fancy in your sandwiches?' I say and make a sharp exit to the kitchen.

I'm early at the cliff steps and decide to call for Meg at the boathouse.

Meg opens the door just a crack. I can barely see her. But there's no doubt about it. Her eyes are furious.

'I told you never to call,' she hisses. 'Go away.'

'What about Willow?' I hiss back. 'You coming?'

'You'll have to look after her today,' she whispers. She goes to close the door, but bony fingers grip the edge. The gap widens. Seth's face looms next to Meg's, his eyes frantic.

'Where's David, laddie? Have ye seen David?'

I shake my head, unsure what to say.

The old man points up at the sky. His finger trembles. 'It's close. It's coming. Tell him, laddie.'

'Come inside, Grandad,' Meg says, her hand on his arm. 'We'll sit down and decide what to do, OK?'

He stares at her for a second, shakes her hand away, pushes his way past me, heads behind the house, where his boat lies like a hidden memory. Like a threat.

Meg follows. 'Go, Luke!' she shouts over her shoulder. 'Just look after Willow. I'll come when I can.'

She doesn't come at all that day. Or the next. Things must be really bad with her grandad. I keep wondering whether to call again, offer to help. But seeing me seems to wind the old man up even more. I don't want to make things worse for him. Or for Meg. And it's not like she wants me there.

There's no news from Dad. Which, I tell myself, is a good thing. And Mum's taking more photos. Albeit close to the cottage.

It *is* strange at the croft without Meg: quiet. No seabird scrutiny. No bubble of laugh. No 'instructions'.

But Willow is great company. We hang out together by the pond. I throw her lunchtime fish into the water to test her diving skills. She brings it to the surface with something very like a smile on her face; sits to eat with one eye fixed on me.

'Don't worry,' I say. 'I'm not a fan of sushi.'

On the second day we venture into the dunes, where Willow discovers that she can slide from top to bottom on her back. She does this over and over. She's hilarious. Full of joy. She makes me feel light as air. I almost join in her game. Maybe next time.

We wander as far as the strip of damp sand where the tide has left its usual pebble and shell gem collection. I worry that Willow might make a dash for the sea, even though the tide is well out when we're there. We might be best of friends now but she's a wild animal. At some point the call of the wild's got to win. Thankfully, she doesn't hear it this time. She isn't ready. Neither am I.

She collects pebbles in her mouth, or lies on her back like a sunbather, juggling one between her front paws. Once she drops a round pink stone at my feet. That's the start of a game of otter fetch that, apparently, she could play forever. After a while, I'm remembering other beach games, games with Dad: burying him up to his neck in sand; him bursting out and chasing me into the sea. Salty chips shared on a sea wall. Dad. Mum. And me. I sit down, keep throwing stones, but Willow loses interest. Or senses something's changed. She wriggles between my knees. Her whiskers tickle my bare knees. She stares, blinks. Sneezes. And I'm laughing again.

We race up and down the dunes until we're both flagging and head back to the croft for a snack: cold pizza for me, more 'sushi' for her. We round off our day with a poolside snooze, Willow on her favourite velvet-covered tree stump, me beside her on the grass. Wearing a thick layer of sun cream.

I'm sorry when the light dulls. I don't want to move.

Willow is wise to my preparing-to-leave routine; runs

back outside as soon as she sees me refill the water bowl in her pen. We play hide-and-seek for at least half an hour, before her stomach gets the better of her and she heads for the fish bucket indoors. I manage to get to it first, and drop the last of the coley inside the pen so that she has no choice but to let me put her inside.

'That's the last fish,' I tell her, as she tears and munches. 'So it's no good shouting for more.'

If Meg doesn't show tomorrow, I'll either knock at her door, or try a solo fishing trip. On balance, the ocean sounds preferable. How hard could it be?

I'm 'a natural boatsman' after all.

My confidence has waned long before I walk through the cottage gate.

Luckily, there's a note taped to the summerhouse door.

See you at the steps tomorrow, city
boy. Usual time.
M
PS Sorry.

When I get indoors, there's been a message from Dad too: Iris's operation went well. But she's still 'recovering'.

'What does that mean?' I ask Mum.

'She's in the best hands, love,' Mum says.

Which means she doesn't know.

I wonder if anyone does, even the doctors.

But, I think, if Iris could talk, she'd say that the hands she needs most are her mum's. And, just maybe, her dad's too.

I hope she knows they're near.

## TWENTY-EIGHT

Willow finds her own breakfast without the need for anyone to set foot in a fishing boat. She plunges into the pool after an unfortunate frog the minute we release her from the croft, settles on a rock to eat it. I'm grateful for the screen of reeds around her. I'm not ready for 'nature' in full Technicolor detail.

'She's doing well,' I tell Meg.

'Proud father,' Meg says.

I smile; feel warm inside.

We clean Willow's pen and wait for her to flop out on her tree stump.

'We'll need to go soon if we're to catch the tide,' Meg says. 'See if she'll follow you indoors.'

Given her hide-and-seek prowess, I'm not hopeful. But this time she trots in through the door at my heels. I look back at Meg. She's impressed, I can tell.

But Willow *won't* go in her pen. She crawls into the back of the fireplace, crouches there with a defiant gleam

in her eye. We give up, decide to leave her with the run of
the croft – which hopefully is not a mistake – and set off
for the high seas. Well, the gentle waves of Puffin Bay . . .

A lone puffin is guarding Billy's boat. A striped flag to
mark the spot. She jumps down as we approach, waddles
to a nearby rock. A racket of gulls follows us as we drag the
boat to the water; squabble among themselves in the air.

The fish take longer to bite today. The gulls drift away
and there's just the roll and splash of the oars, the distant
roar of the serious waves further out to sea. Something
about the still blue space makes me pick up our
conversation where we left it last time.

'Iris,' I say. 'She's called Iris. My sister.' The word
feels softer in my mouth now; a better fit. The sharp
edges are gone.

Meg looks up from her rod, smiles. 'How's she doing?'

'I don't know,' I say. 'They had to do something to her
heart.' I stare towards the dark strip of land on the horizon:
the mainland, where miles of road lie between me and Iris.
The still blue space of the sea seems suddenly too wide.

Then I think of Dad and Jenny beside the plastic

hospital cot, hands clutched tightly together. I don't see room for me.

Resentment pinches, cold and hard in my stomach. I try to will it away. Iris didn't ask to be born. And right now, I think, she needs Dad even more than I do.

My fishing line twitches. I jump, almost drop the rod, have to tense my fingers around the handle.

'False alarm,' Meg says. 'You OK?'

I shrug. 'Fine,' I say.

The seabird eyes hover on mine. In the clear, uncluttered light I notice purple smudges beneath them. I hesitate, wonder whether to ask.

'Your turn,' I say.

'Sorry?'

'Your turn to talk. If you want.' I hold her blue gaze. The edges blur with sea and sky. 'Ocean confession and all that. Might help.'

A whip of wind pulls at her hair, drops it across her face. There's a new metallic scent in the air. 'Bit of a squall coming,' she says, squinting at the end of her line. It lifts, drops. 'Hope we get a bite in a minute. We'll have to get back before it builds.'

She sighs. 'August is hard for Grandad,' she says. 'It's when we lost Mum and Dad.' She trails her hand over the side of the boat again, into the sea that stole them both. Her face softens, as if she might still reach them there. 'And it's when the weather starts to turn,' she says. 'It's like there's this confused bit between summer sun and the real harshness of an island winter; a sort "boiling pot", folk around here say, where anything can happen.' She pulls her hand from the water like it's been bitten. 'August is when it comes. If it's going to.' She looks up at me again. 'The Otters' Moon.'

Our lines tug and twist. Game on.

We're rowing to shore with a small catch of mackerel when she finally explains about the rare moon that stole her parents; the pale spectral moon that throws enough light only for the most skilled of night hunters: the otter.

'Not a time to be out at sea unless you're one of them,' Meg says. 'Because there's worse to come. On the night of an Otters' Moon, when darkness is at its thickest, a blinding mist rolls in – or, rather, drops in from nowhere. It ushers in a weird isolated storm that stays in the sea; never reaches the sky or shore.' She shifts on the wooden bench. Specks of moisture glisten on her cheeks. Perhaps sea spray. Perhaps not. 'Not many people live to tell the tale,' she says. 'But those that do mention strange lights, strange sounds; strange colours swirling around them. Trying to get inside.'

I shiver. Struggle for words. This isn't all island fiction, or the ramblings of a sad old man. Meg's parents died under an Otters' Moon. You don't get more real than that.

'Thank you,' I say. 'For telling me.'

We reach the shallows, have to jump ankle-deep into the water, pull the boat on to the sand. I'm still trying to decide whether it's all right to ask more questions when we're done.

What *exactly* happened under that treacherous Otters' Moon? How did it get the better of both Meg's parents? And why does Seth think it's about to return . . .?

Meg is silent as we heave the boat to the anchor post. Maybe she needs the mystery. Maybe that's a softer place to fall when you lose both your parents in one night. No clear answers: no clear pictures to haunt you.

I risk just one.

'So there's no explanation,' I say, 'you know, for this strange moon; the weird weather that comes with it? Surely scientists or someone –'

She knots the rope around the anchor post, pulls it tight. 'Maybe,' she says eventually. 'But what difference would it make?' She brushes sand from her shins, rolls down the legs of her dungarees. Her eyes meet mine, misted like the Otters' Moon. 'No scientist in the world can bring back Mum and Dad. *Or* stop my grandad losing bits of himself every single day.'

'I'm really sorry, Meg,' I say. 'For all of it.'

I retrieve my trainers from behind a rock and pull them on. Sand scratches the soles of my feet and ankles. I take them off again, try to brush it away.

'My mum,' I say, '*she's* a bit lost too.' I clear my throat. There seems to be sand in there as well.

Meg nods. 'I guessed.' She rests her hand on my arm. 'There'll be a way back for her, city boy.'

I nod, brush my cheek with a gritty hand. 'Yes,' I say. 'There will be.'

Maybe, just maybe, I think, Mum has found the start of it here on this island. Maybe, somehow, she knew where to come.

'But Grandad,' Meg says, 'he'll just keep drifting further and further away. And soon no one will be able to find him. Not even me.'

We sit a while among the pebbles, shoulders touching, and stare out to sea.

Willow has created an isolated storm of her own back at the croft. Upturned furniture, a deluge of bath water and scratches on the back door worthy of a caged tiger.

'Missed us, did you?' I say.

'She might have been unsettled by the threatening squall. Animals sense changes in the air long before we do.' Meg looks round at the chaos. 'We can't hold her much longer,' she says. 'She needs her freedom.'

'Not yet,' I say. 'She still needs *us* more.'

Willow makes a leap for the kitchen table, helps herself to a fresh mackerel from the bucket.

'That's the last of your fast-food meals, Willow,' Meg says. 'From here on you work for it.'

Willow chitters through her mouthful of fin and flesh, scatters scale sequins into the air.

'And no answering back,' Meg says.

Meg and I are starving too. Our cheese-sandwich lunch has survived the otter storm only because Meg thought to hide it in the tumbledown outhouse. A family of ants clings to the first one I unwrap. I eat it, anyway. Minus the ants.

The squall is quickly over, nothing more than a few gusts of wind and a sprinkle of rain by the time it makes it to land. We walk back across the dunes, wait while Willow does a triathlon of sand slides, pebble juggling and rockpool dives.

The tide is further in. Willow invents a new game: chase the wave. In, out, in, out, she goes, like a nervous bather. Sea froth gathers in her whiskers.

Meg and I paddle, enjoy the coolness of the water on our ankles. Willow follows.

Suddenly, she tenses. She plunges further in, dives with a flick of her tail in the air. Disappears.

My heart thuds. I scan the waves.

'Where is she?' I say. 'What if she doesn't come back?'

'Then she *is* ready to leave,' Meg says. She walks out of the water, sits down on the sand, knees under her chin. 'Or she might be testing herself, like she would if her mum was with her. Let's see what happens.'

Sure enough, the flat head soon appears, riding the waves. Willow emerges with a small white fish clamped between her jaws. She runs towards us, drops it at my feet; squeaks and whistles in what is clearly otter pride.

I feel ridiculously proud, too. I think of Jez and his mad terrier, Dizzy. How he taught her to 'play dead' and give high fives. How he glowed about it like he was the clever one. *Now* I get it.

'Well done, Willow,' I say. 'You're a sea fisherman . . . woman.'

'Person,' Meg says.

We flop back on the sand, laughing far more than the moment warrants. It feels good. Willow shakes half of the ocean out of her coat and into our faces, then removes herself to a flat-topped rock, turns her back on us, and begins the serious business of eating.

We laugh some more.

'Next time,' Meg says, as we wander back to the croft, 'we should take Willow out in the boat. See how she copes in deeper water. We could head for Lighthouse Rock, let her explore a bit. As long as the weather stays quiet.'

Visions of hungry wide-mouthed seals and soaring eagles fall into my head.

'*Suppose*,' I say.

But when we leave for home, I look up into the clouds and pray for several days of *serious* squalls.

'There's your grandad,' I say. 'By the cliff steps.'

He spots us as we come further round the bay, adjusts a bundle of driftwood under his arm, waves.

'Beachcombing,' Meg says. 'He's having a good day today.'

'He's limping. Is he hurt?'

'Shrapnel fragments in his knee. It plays up sometimes. The weather affects that too.'

The war wound.

'He was a soldier?' I say.

'Navy,' Meg says. 'For a time. Don't get him started on that or you'll never go home.' She smiles. 'He talks of it more and more these days; the camaraderie. The dramas. The friends he lost.'

His face lights up as we come close, creases into a smile just like Meg's. All the memories he can't catch, all the battles he can't forget, are there in the weather-beaten skin, the folds and crevices. Today the wild blue-eyed boy peers out from among them again.

I smile back at him.

'C'mon in, laddie,' he says. 'I ike tae have a go at that carving again?'

I hesitate, loath to disappoint him. 'Tomorrow?' I say. 'Would that be OK? Only Mum's expecting me.'

He nods. 'Good lad,' he says. 'Tomorrow, then. Catherine here'll give ye some lunch, eh, lass?'

I shoot Meg a glance, raise an eyebrow. This is a *good* day?

'Same time in the morning,' she whispers, with a quick nod in the direction of the steps. 'If I can. Then we'll see.'

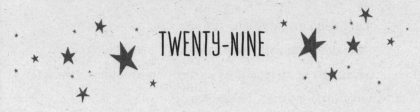

# TWENTY-NINE

I put my head round Mum's bedroom door to tell her I'm off to meet Meg. She's sitting up in bed, laptop open on her knee.

'I got some good shots yesterday,' she says. 'Interesting new light. Want to see?'

'Please,' I say. Because the light in her eyes is new too. She really *does* seem to be getting better. Meg will have to wait for me for once. She can hardly complain.

She does.

It's humid this morning still. No sign of my hoped-for squalls. But Meg's face is a perfect storm. Her hair clings to her forehead in damp spirals; her cheeks are red. 'Do you know how hard it is for me to get away?' she says. 'I can't be hanging around waiting for you.' Lightning flashes across the seabird eyes. 'And nor can Willow.'

I'm fifteen minutes late. If that.

'Bad morning with your grandad?' I say.

She grabs her bag, slings it over one shoulder. 'I'm not leaving him for long.' She strides off.

I hurry after her. 'No wood carving for me, then?'

She sighs. 'Who knows?' she says. 'But the sooner we get Willow back into the wild, the better. I need to stay close to home.' Her shoulders drop. Her bag slides down her arm. The fire is gone.

'You can't do this on your own, Meg. It's too hard. Maybe if I told Mum . . .'

'No! Don't you dare.'

I hold up my palms. 'It's just . . . there might be something to help him. I mean, you don't know . . .'

'No, *you* don't know,' she hisses. 'Now come on. Unless you fancy taking Willow out to sea on your own, we need to do it now.'

I trudge alongside her, already hot and uncomfortable. The air is thick, a heavy syrup in my chest. The sun is a weird, intense pinhead on the horizon.

Everything feels wrong.

I've got a bad feeling about today. I don't want Willow in that boat.

A bead of sweat runs down my nose. I shove my hands in my jean pockets, hoping for a tissue to wipe it away. My fingers find a hole in the bottom of the left one. Something round and smooth has slipped through into the lining. One of Willow's play pebbles. I wriggle it free, close my palm tightly around it.

I make a show of wiping my arm across my forehead. 'Sun's glaring,' I say. 'It'll be unbearable in that boat. I don't see why we can't just let Willow play on the beach like we did yesterday. Let her build her sea skills in her own time.' I glance at Meg's face. Sweat beads cluster on her nose too. 'And you could use a rest.'

Meg stops, hands on hips. Her 'no point in arguing' stance. 'I'm taking her out,' she says. 'Come with us. Don't come with us. Please yourself, city boy.'

'That's rich,' I say. 'In case you've forgotten, I'm the one who's done most of the babysitting. Otter-sitting. You don't get to just overrule me on this.'

'Yep, I do,' she says, chin jutting forward. 'I'm the one who decided to take her from the wild. It's my job to make sure she gets back there.'

'You're rushing her. I know her better than you do. She's

not ready for the ocean, for everything that's out there. I can look after her myself if you're tied up with your grandad. She still needs me.'

'And what about when you go back to your city-boy life? School starts soon, doesn't it? What happens then to a wild creature that doesn't know how to be fully wild?' She looks me square in the eyes. 'She's an otter, Luke. Not your baby sister.'

Willow is raring to go, oblivious to the tension between Meg and me. She races ahead of us as we untie the boat. No time for a triathlon today. I can't see her when we emerge from the dunes, worry that I've already lost her to the wild.

It's another game of hide-and-seek. She leans out from behind a rock, shoots behind it when she sees us.

'Coming, ready or not,' I shout. I leave Meg with the boat, follow Willow as she scurries from one hiding place to another with a series of excited squeaks and yips.

I'm soon out of breath. Otters might not be as graceful on land as they are in water, but they're seriously fast on their feet.

Meg has dragged the boat to the shoreline. She's sitting inside, stony-faced.

I know the look; know the burn of pain behind it, unrelenting as the August sun. I want to help her, throw cool water on the flames, but today the gap between us is wider than the sky.

She pulls a grey fish from the bucket and holds it up. Willow scrambles into the boat. Meg jumps out, pushes it forward until the lift of the waves takes over. I don't even have time to roll up my jeans. I run into the water and swing myself over the side. I give what I hope is a decent evil seabird stare of my own. Meg looks away. I take up my oar and start to row.

The sea flattens as we go further out; shimmers like green bottle glass in the sun. Rowing gets harder, like I'm pulling against the might of the whole ocean. Willow rides with her front paws on the rim of the boat, eyes glued to the waters beneath. Her head darts from side to side as something catches her attention there. She's riveted.

The lighthouse grows larger in front of us, throws a rippling replica of itself on to the waves. Its rocky base is more impressive than it appears from the shore: craggy and sharp, raven-black in places, silver and green where lichen or limpets have colonised it. Waves curl around the base, giving glimpses of underwater rocks that protrude like treacherous teeth. I think of Meg's grandad, out here in the dark, under that Otters' Moon, searching for his son; how he's in treacherous seas all over again. Still searching.

That's some kind of love.

'We jump out in a minute and walk the boat in,' Meg says. 'There's an anchor point. Follow me, or you'll slash your feet on the rocks.'

I look at her, re-focus; nod. 'Perfect,' I say.

Willow glides effortlessly between rocks. Meg and I pick our way towards a shale-covered landing space in a fork in the rock. A sloped launch pad leads into the ocean to one side of it, and above that rough-hewn steps lead up to the lighthouse itself. Meg ties the boat to a metal post, using several careful knots.

'Explore the lighthouse if you want,' she says. 'I'll keep an eye on Willow. You'll find bottled water in the old kitchen. My stash.'

I shake my head. 'No, thanks,' I say, although I'd love to see inside. I'm not ready for an olive branch. And I'm not leaving Willow with Meg. Not today.

'Suit yourself. *I'll* get the water.'

I sit halfway up the staircase, watch Willow's antics in the sea. She tumbles and turns, leaps and dives, each dive lasting longer than the previous one. There are no telltale rings, no silver bubbles to mark her position on the shifting surface of the sea. I hold my breath each time she disappears, feet first, tail lashing; breathe again when I see the whiskered nose.

She takes a short break next to me on the shale, then uses the boat launch pad as a freestyle slide into the waves. She knows how to have fun. I wish I could join her.

When Meg arrives with the water, Willow greets her with a fat pink fish between her teeth.

'Salmon,' Meg says. 'Good choice.'

Willow settles beside us on the shale to enjoy her catch.

'So, OK, you're right,' I say, ignoring a tiny twinge of sadness. 'She's at home here; she can feed herself. But there's a gang of greedy predators out there, ready to snap up a tender otter takeaway. She's still an easy target. You said so yourself.'

Meg gives a wry smile. 'We can't protect her forever.'

'So what, we just leave her here?'

'No. We take her back to the forest, by the croft. She can fish in the pond, swim in the burn; head for the beach – brave the sea – when she wants to. She has her boltholes.' She scoops up a handful of shale, lets it slide through her fingers. 'She's stronger now. We've given her a chance. It's the best we can do.'

She kneels up. 'Tide's drawing out,' she says. 'Time to go.'

She nods at Willow, who is curled up, heavy-eyed after her salmon feast, ready for a nap. 'See if you can get her into the boat before she gets a second wind,' she says. 'I'll untie it.'

As I get to my feet, a dark winged reflection spreads across the shale. We look up at the sky.

'Eagle,' Meg says. 'Get hold of Willow.'

Willow has seen it too. She stiffens. Struggles from my grasp.

And before I can stop her, she plunges from the rocks into the sea.

We dash to the edge. The waves have closed over her. We yell her name, but our voices disappear.

The eagle hovers; sails low. We jump up and down, flap our arms in the air, make as much noise as we can. His great claws hang over our heads like the undercarriage of an invading aircraft. His yellow searchlight eyes are on us for a moment, then he dismisses us with a slow turn of his head; lands, hunches his shoulders and peers down into the water.

My heart bangs against my ribs; blood fizzes in my ears. How much longer before Willow needs to come up for air?

I pick up my empty water bottle and lob it at his feet. He gives it – and me – a disinterested glance. His eyes narrow. He lifts back into the air, his vast wings stirring the shale around us. His dark shadow spreads over the sea.

'He *is* awesome,' Meg says.

I swing round. 'What's wrong with you?' I shout. 'Willow's out there all alone – with that . . . killing machine. And it's *totally* because of you.'

# THIRTY

'If we don't go now,' Meg says. 'We'll be marooned here. Unless you a fancy walking back across the mudflats. And the sinking sand beneath them.'

She's right, I know. The tide is pulling back strongly, the tooth-like rocks more exposed beneath my vantage point. I cup my hands around my mouth and call one more time.

Willow isn't coming back.

I climb into the boat, take up my oar. I feel stiff, as ancient as the ocean. The weight in my chest is enough to take us to its murky depths in seconds.

I can't look at Meg.

We row in silence with only the screech of the wooden oars against their metal loops, the slap of sea against the hull for company. Willow's river-deep stare is in every splash of light on water; her call in each whistle – every whisper of the wind. It feels like the eagle has his talons deep under my ribs.

When we heave the boat ashore, I see that Meg's eyes are red and swollen from crying.

I walk away.

Mum is coming out of the front door as I arrive at the cottage. 'I looked in the cupboards,' she says. 'Thought I'd better go to the shop. Want to come with me? We could choose something interesting for dinner.'

'They don't have anything interesting,' I say. 'Unless you're a fan of antique tinned steak. Anyway, I'm not hungry.'

She peers into my face, moves a strand of hair from my forehead. 'Are you OK?'

I shrug, struggle with the push of tears.

'Maybe Mr Campbell would let you use his phone: you could try and get hold of your dad, ask what's happening with the baby.'

'You ring, Mum,' I say through gritted teeth. I squeeze past her into the hallway, 'Ask him about Iris, yeah. And while you're at it, ask him exactly why he just cleared off and abandoned his first child.'

I go to my room, throw myself face down on my bed. Meg's bed.

The smell of fish and sea air floats from my T-shirt. I get up, throw it in the wash basket and reach into my wardrobe for another. I spot the remains of Dad's red guitar at the bottom next to some folded blankets. Mum must have put it there, thinking it was too precious to throw away. I scoop the pieces into my arms, carry them downstairs and out to the bin by the back door. I look at them for a moment, lying there among potato peelings and the wrappers from last night's frozen pizzas. I close the lid. Some things just can't be fixed.

I lie on my back, watch a bluebottle banging pointlessly against the windowpane. I put my head under the pillow and try to escape into sleep.

The tears come, anyway. For Willow. For Mum. For Iris. For Meg and her lost grandfather.

For me.

I sense movement near my feet and emerge, blinking. Mum is sitting there, her face flushed with sun and crumpled with concern. She holds out a glass of squash. Drops of condensation slide down the side on to her fingers.

'I got hold of your dad,' she says.

I sit up, rub my eyes, reach for the drink. 'Thanks,' I say. My hand shakes a little. There's the clink of ice. 'So?'

Mum sighs. 'He only had a minute,' she says. 'They were in a flap. Iris has an infection. He was upset. He said he was sorry.'

'Sorry for himself, most likely,' I mutter.

Mum puts her hand around mine. For once hers is the steadier of the two. The ice in my glass stops rattling. 'We should go home, Luke. Take you to the hospital.'

'Did Dad say that?' I ask.

'No. But I think he wanted to.'

'You're doing it again, Mum. Making excuses for him. Don't bother. He's not ruining your break. You were right about this place. You need to stay.'

She gets to her feet. 'This isn't about me,' she says. 'Or your dad. It's about you meeting your sister.' She looks into my face. 'Iris is very poorly, Luke. You do understand that?'

'She'll be OK, though?' I say.

'I'm not sure, sweetheart. That's why I think we should go.'

I rest my glass carefully on the bedside table, study the delicate slivers of melting ice in the bottom. 'When?' I say. 'Not now?'

The thought of leaving the island – of an entire ocean and half another country between Willow and me – it's too much to bear. Too final.

But then there's Iris . . .

'The next ferry is tomorrow morning. I booked us on while I was at the shop,' Mum says.

'No, Mum,' I shout. 'I'll go. But I'm *not* going yet. Not tomorrow.'

'Sweetheart, I know this is difficult. It is for me, too. But Iris . . . We're going tomorrow. It's the best thing –'

'I *said* I'll go. But you don't get to tell me when. You. Dad. Meg. Everyone. I'm sick of you all telling me what's best. According to Dad, him *leaving* us was "for the *best*"; things would "settle down". According to the sacred Jenny, me having a new sibling would be "*good for us as a family*". According to *you*, this island holiday would be a tonic for us both. Look how well all that worked out!'

Mum picks up my empty glass. 'The island,' she says. 'It *has* helped *me*.'

'Yeah,' I say. 'But not enough.'

I stuff my head back under the pillow, already

ashamed of that last remark.

Mum presses her hand on my leg. 'We leave tomorrow,' she says again, her voice flatter now. 'Because we have to. For you. You'll see that one day.'

The hand moves away. 'I'll start tidying this place after we've eaten,' she says, lifting her voice an octave or two. 'Help very welcome.'

Even from under my pillow, I hear the bravery in that shift.

She goes downstairs to start dinner. I won't be able to stomach a thing.

I emerge, kneel up; punch the pillow until feathers drift in the air. I pace the room. I think of Iris, trapped in her incubator, waiting for her fragile heart to heal. Of Willow, trapped between sea and sky and the searing eyes of an eagle. Waiting for me to find her.

And I decide. For myself.

Tomorrow I go to the mainland for Iris.

But tonight I go back to Lighthouse Rock. For Willow.

I open the window and waft the bluebottle through the gap to freedom.

# THIRTY-ONE

I go downstairs and force down sausage and mash. I'll need energy for my mission. I wash up the dinner things, excuse myself from cleaning duty until the morning. I want to say my goodbyes to Meg now, I tell Mum. She nods, smiles, says she's proud of me for being so mature. I feel a stab of guilt. But I *have* to do this.

I set off at five thirty. If I'm to make it to the rock and back before dark, there's no time to lose.

I hesitate as I reach the cliff steps. Meg is the last person I want to see. But can I really manage Billy's boat on my own? I turn towards the boathouse.

The door is wide open, swinging on its hinges. I knock. No answer.

I step inside. The place is silent. There's no one here.

I can't afford to wait. And, in any case, this whole thing with Willow is Meg's fault. I'm best going ahead with my rescue plan on my own.

Billy's boat is waiting, nestled in the sand. I throw my

bag inside, congratulate myself on my supplies: water, sandwich, torch; tin of tuna for Willow; a thick towel to wrap her in. Just in case. A waterproof jacket for me.

I loop the anchor rope over my shoulder and under my arm, as Meg taught me; drag the boat out of the dunes and head towards the shore.

I forgot about the tide.

The sea is still well out. I remember the treacherous rock teeth, the submerged sinking sand. I can move the boat a bit further towards the shoreline, but then I'll just have to wait.

I settle in the bottom of the hull, arms behind my head, feet up on the seat that earlier held Meg. The sun is low and still warm. I watch clouds scud across the sky, the purposeful plod-peck of oystercatchers on the sand. I listen to the chatter of puffins, carried on the wind. Gulls wheel and cry. I close my eyes.

I wake to a cool breeze on my skin and the hiss of the ocean. The beach is deserted now, not a single bird to be seen. The sun has dipped out of sight, too. But I can see the loom of Lighthouse Rock in the water. The striped finger of the lighthouse itself cuts through the round face of the moon –which, strangely, casts little light on to the waves.

It's much later than I'd intended.

But this is my only chance. Willow might be out there, waiting for me. She might be injured. Afraid.

I *have* to try.

Lone rowing is harder than I expected. The oars are heavy. I struggle to coordinate the movement of the two together, waste useless minutes bobbing in circles, getting nowhere.

My arms are already tired. I'm falling at the first hurdle.

Then, suddenly, I have it. The boat surges forward, pushed by a tail wind that has come out of nowhere. As long as I concentrate, I might actually do this. I'm on a roll.

I keep my eyes fixed on the lighthouse, keep my breathing steady.

The sea darkens to inky blue. The moon lifts higher in the sky: a luminous, staring eye.

Muscles tighten across my chest. A sharp pain shoots down my arm. I relax my grip on one oar for a split second, just as a wave surges like a great whale. It buffets the boat, lifts it from underneath. The oar flies from my hand.

I lean over the side, manage to heave it back into the boat before it's tossed out of reach. I struggle to refind my rowing rhythm; struggle to catch my breath.

I can't let that happen again.

The lighthouse seems to sway in front of me. Should I

turn back? I look over my shoulder for the safety of Puffin Bay. I can barely make it out. I've travelled further out than I thought. Better to keep going. Willow might be just as scared as I am.

I focus on the turn of the oars, count them like beats in a bar of music. The lighthouse grows larger, but its edges blur. It's black stripes fade. I should have eaten more before setting out. Once I reach the rock, I'll need my sandwiches. I push and pull harder on the oars.

The darkness thickens. My eyelids become heavy. It's harder still to focus on my destination. I squeeze my eyes shut, open them again. Misted shapes drift across the face of the moon, wrap around it like a ghostly veil, block its pale light. An icy wind curls around my neck and arms. What's going on with the weather?

The boat stirs underneath me, tilts and starts to turn. There's a rush of sound: a roar of waves. A sheet of slicing rain blinds me, steals my breath. The oars slide in my cold, wet hands. I cling on to them, try desperately to fight the spin of the sea.

I lose.

What was I thinking, coming out here alone? Fear crawls around my neck. My heart pounds against my ribs.

The waves snatch both oars. They smack into the side

of the hull, whirl in the water. One of them rears in the air above me, threatens to come down on my head.

The lighthouse has disappeared.

Grey tendrils of mist twist around me. Odd lights, in colours I can't name, creep across the swirling surface of the sea and reach towards me. The moon glows a ghostly pale green.

This is it. The Otters' Moon.

Old Seth was right.

He said it was coming. And he said it was coming for *me*.

I curl into a ball, put my hands over my head. The boat spins faster. My heart leaps and thuds in my ears. The nameless colours swirl inside my head. Iris's indigo eyes flicker among them; Willow's silver bubbles float and fade. I feel like I'm breathing through a straw.

'I'm sorry,' I whisper. To both of them.

To Mum. To Meg.

I start to drift like the mist, light and barely real.

The boat rears in the air. The sea surges around me, sucks me down. The ocean thunders in my ears, gurgles in my throat. I gasp and splutter, flail and kick, brought back into reality by the icy shock. I surface, gulp in salt air, try to swim.

It's hopeless. My arms are no match for the waves;

I have no sense of where I am or where I'm going. Cold grips me, anchors me to the spot. I start to sink.

Something barges against my chest, slithers warm around my neck. Something nudges at the back of my knees. Something bristled moves under my hand. The water around my face vibrates with sound.

Selkies. Come to steal my human soul.

Not just a story, after all.

The barging continues.

There is pain somewhere. A sharp nip. Perhaps in my toe. Wiry whiskers brush my face. Claws scratch at my clothes. Let them do their worst. Get it over with. I'm limp now, numb with cold and fear, no fight left in me.

The sea pauses for a moment. I float upwards. As my ears break the surface, I hear it. A thin three-note lament.

Willow?

I suck in a huge breath of air, kick my feet, thrash my arms in from of me, try to stay afloat. My sodden clothes and heavy trainers drag me down.

It *is* Willow. I know her in my bones.

She rides the waves, circles around me, swims below me, nips at my ankles. She chitters anxiously every time my face bobs below the waves. Her tail lashes my cheek. Adrenaline shoots through my veins, wakens my limbs.

My body finds a remembered rhythm. I swim. Somehow, I swim, led by the whip of Willow's tail; the forward thrust of her strong hindquarters. Every time I falter, she stops, hangs in the water in front of me, nips my nose or an ear.

Then there's the sharp snatch of rock; the skitter of stones. Willow's river-deep stare comes in and out of focus from above me. Whistles and screams rise above the wind and the drumbeat in my ears.

She plunges back into the sea. Bites at the neck of my sweatshirt, tears at my sleeve. I heave myself upwards and collapse – on to dry land. My fingers grasp at its gritty, sliding surface. Shale.

Lighthouse Rock.

It has to be.

Willow has rescued *me*.

# THIRTY-TWO

I open my eyes to clear blue space and the drift of a single white bird. I try to follow it.

My head swims, thumps with pain. My arms and legs are stiff, icy cold. But there's a warm, soothing weight on my chest. Right above my heart.

I ease my shoulders from the ground. My chin meets thick, soft fur. Round moon eyes lift to mine. And I remember.

Willow chitters, slides away from me and disappears behind a ledge. She returns with a silver fish, very much past its best, lays it on my knee. Breakfast. Meg isn't the only one with a stash on Lighthouse Rock.

I smooth Willow's long back, try to replay the events of the night. They shift and sway like the morning sea beneath us. But one thing is crystal clear. If it wasn't for Willow, the last thing I'd have seen of this world would have been the cold, cruel stare of an Otter's Moon. I scoop her closer, bury my face against her strong neck. Willow stills, presses against me. I don't need to speak otter. She knows.

I sit up, ease her on to my knee. 'What now, then, Willow?' I say.

Her muscles tense under my hand. Fur bristles on the back of her neck. She looks up.

Not the eagle again. Please. Not now.

I follow her gaze. A black speck cuts its way through the sky, grows larger. I see a tail. A bulbous body. A deep sound, a kind of whirling hum, grows slowly louder. A shadow spreads across the new sun; darkens the waves, looms lower and lower.

Not a bird. A helicopter.

Its great blade spins; stirs the air and the sea and the shale beneath us. An arm lifts in greeting. The craft swings to one side, prepares to land.

Willow rears on her hind legs.

'It's OK,' I say.

She stares her wise stare. Sings her three-note song.

This time it's a goodbye.

I stroke her head one last time.

'Bye, Willow,' I say.

She blinks her eyes, turns and leaps gracefully from Lighthouse Rock into the frothing white waves beneath.

Mum jumps from the helicopter with a yellow-clad

paramedic. She runs towards me, her hair whipping madly in the downdraught. She wraps me in a thick blanket, scoops me in her arms. Today they are surprisingly strong.

'How did you know?' I say through chattering teeth.

'I didn't,' she says. 'Meg's grandad did. He insisted someone was lost at sea, nearly got himself lost too by all accounts. Meg found him roaming somewhere called Puffin Bay, shouting about a missing boat. She called the coast guard. And then she came banging on our door.' She smiles, dabs at her eyes. 'With a story about some brave city boy, a lighthouse and a wild island otter.'

At the hospital she has more to say. She can't decide who she's most angry with: me, for nearly dying, or herself for letting it happen. Once I've been checked over for broken bones, she won't stop hugging me. It's embarrassing after a while, but I say nothing. There are a lot of hugs to catch up on.

'I made you a promise,' she says, 'while you were out there.'

I look into her eyes. They look steadily back into mine. 'It's OK, Mum,' I say. 'Those things I said, I was just –'

Her hand rests on my chest, butterfly gentle. She shakes her head. 'I made a promise,' she says, 'that if they found *you*, I would find *my* way home, too.' She smiles. 'I'm going to get help, Luke. See someone about my depression. It's stolen enough from me. And from you.'

I take Mum's hand, wrap my stiff fingers around it. 'We'll do it together, Mum,' I say. 'Another mission.'

'This one's down to me, sweetheart,' she says, and smiles and cries and hugs me all over again.

Dad calls twice while I'm waiting to be discharged, anxious to check I'm none the worse for my 'ordeal by Otters' Moon'. His voice cracks. He tells me he's proud of me. Maybe he means it. We'll see.

He says Iris has 'turned the corner' overnight. My sister has weathered her own storm.

She's a survivor. Like Willow. Like me.

Mum rearranges our return ferry to give me time to recuperate. Even though I feel fine. I sleep through until the next morning and then, at last, Meg calls by. She sits on the end of the bed that used to be hers and I tell her my own story of Puffin Bay and an Otters' Moon.

I tell her that her grandad was right.

'Quite an adventure for a city boy,' she says. Then she cries, too.

'Your mum and I talked a lot,' she says when the tears stop. 'About Grandad. She's finding out about special help for him. For us. Here. On the island. At least for now.' She looks down at her hands, looks up again. Smiles. 'She's amazing.'

'I know,' I say, and hold her gaze for a moment. 'You're not so bad yourselves, you and your grandad. At times.' I grin. 'Now get off my bed. There's somewhere we need to go.'

We take Mum to see Puffin Bay.

We stop by Billy's croft, rest by Willow's pool. Mum and Meg talk, heads bent together while I laze in my usual grassy patch of shade. Their voices drift towards me, warm and kind: something about a shared pinkie promise.

Mum walks across and settles beside me. She has another message from Dad. A surprise. He and Jenny wonder if I'd choose a middle name for Iris.

I nod. 'Easy,' I say. 'I choose Willow.'

'Iris Willow.' Mum smiles. 'How beautiful. I'm sure they'll love it.'

Meg joins us; perches on Willow's tree stump couch.

Her seabird eyes are soft today. And blue. Gentle summer-sky blue.

The three of us stare through yellow flag flowers into the pool. Perfect silver bubbles rise to the surface. They drift slowly across the sun-spangled water towards the mossy bank, where a dragonfly hovers on vivid, vibrating wings.

# ACKNOWLEDGEMENTS

This story has emerged over quite a few years, beginning as something different all together. Parts of it were written during stormy and disorienting times. Many people guided and supported me in bringing this final version to shore, casting light on murky waters, or redirecting the boat when it was needed. My heartfelt thanks go to:

My agent, Emily Talbot, at United Agents: for always being there; for being wonderful. What a find you were. Without your proactive support and understanding ear, this book – and its author – might still be drifting in the fog.

Lindsey Heaven at Egmont, for crying (in a good way!) when I pitched my ideas; for your love of otters. For trusting in my ability to write a second book . . .

Jenny Glencross, for your enthusiasm and sympathetic yet incisive edits. For knowing that *Otters' Moon* is about much more than otters. This book is all the better for your suggestions.

Lucy Courtenay, for your warmth and ability to, very

kindly, make me row my boat a little faster than I thought I could. Also, the numerous others at Egmont for all your hard work and key contributions.

Emphatically, to Keith Robinson, for the creation of a cover that is not only beautiful, but reflective of the emotional heart of this story, and the feel and atmosphere of Luke and Meg's island. Such talent. I am so lucky to have you on board.

My friends – you know who you are – for being you, for distracting me from myself, for believing in me. Always.

My lovely teaching colleagues and creative writing students at Bath Spa University, for the constant inspiration, learning, and sense of community.

And – saving the most important until last: my beautiful, brave, creative, and hilarious family: my children, Ali, Joe, Josh, Emma and Oli, grandsons Luca and Jules, my 'daughters-in-law', Kristen, Lyndy, Emily and Phoebe. Where are the words? Here goes:

You shine silver-bright in the centre of everything: my very own Lighthouse Rock. Without you all, I – and my stories – would be lost at sea.